CRUDE CARRIER

A Touchstone Agency Mystery

D0376334

REX BURNS

MYSTERIOUSPRESS.COM

OPEN ROAD
INTEGRATED MEDIA
NEW YORK

CRUDE
CARRIER

Cover design by Kat Lee

978-1-4976-4154-9

Published in 2014 by MysteriousPress.com/Open Road Integrated Media, Inc.
345 Hudson Street
New York, NY 10014
www.mysteriouspress.com
www.openroadmedia.com

To Susan Weston-Frey
1949–2009

CRUDE CARRIER

I

It all started with a letter from the owners of the SS *Aurora Victorious* to the parents of the ship's third officer:

Hercules Maritime Shipping Company, Ltd.
Sea Transport of General and Specialized Cargo
Home Office: 17 Crosswall St., London, EC3
Agencies in New York, Yokohama, Brindisi,
Fremantle, Abu Dhabi

Mr. and Mrs. R. A. Rossi
22390 Belleview Lane
Denver, Colorado 80209
USA

Dear Mr. and Mrs. Rossi,
    It is with deep regret that we inform you of the death at sea of your son, Third Officer Harold Rossi, aboard

the SS Aurora Victorious. *Enclosed, please find a check for the amount of US$3,027.14, the total of Third Officer Rossi's due wages and allowances, less deductions and fees.*

Please understand that Hercules Maritime Shipping Company, Ltd., has been absolved of any legal responsibility for your son's death. If you have further questions, please do not hesitate to contact one of our offices.

With sincere condolences,
Joseph K. Wood
Marine Superintendent

JKW:ml
  (Encl.)

Subsequent attempts by Mr. and Mrs. Rossi to reach one of those offices and ask further questions about the death of their son had been fruitless. Their frustration led, one warm September afternoon, to the offices of the Touchstone Agency and the desk of James Raiford.

The Rossis had only three letters they could show Raiford. Most of their communication with their son had been by telephone or by camcorder discs that were usually erased and refilmed. The letters spoke of ports of call: loading at oil platforms in the Persian Gulf—well south, Rossi assured his parents, of Iraq and its turmoil—and unloading at the Virgin Islands in the Gulf of Mexico. One envelope bore a bright stamp from St. Croix, Virgin Islands, while the other two had Arabic stamps. The earliest letter stated that Third Mate Rossi disliked the fact that the oil tanker was so big they had to load and unload far from shore—sometimes as much as fifty miles out. But if his first ship—the MV *Helena Georgiou*, according to his parents—was more fun in port, the pay and living conditions were much better on a tanker, even one so old. The second letter said he was learning a lot about ships in general and oil tankers in particular, since the *Aurora Victorious* was so automated that the small crew had to tend to all duties above- and belowdecks. He also described a big storm they went through north of Madagascar, and he offered one line on Halul Island: "sort of like a flattened biscuit, real hot, with a lot of oil transfer rigs." He said he would send another disc when enough worth taking pictures of happened. The last letter spoke of shipboard routine and dislike for the first mate. All were filled with questions about home: what was happening and who was doing it.

They also gave Raiford a copy of Rossi's contract, which he'd sent home for safekeeping. A boilerplate document, its blanks were filled with Rossi's name, the name of the ship, the duration of the contract, and his monthly salary. Listed in general terms were the duties of the third officer (Navigation) and benefits and allowances that Hercules Maritime would provide in addition to salary. Those benefits, headed "Medical Benefits," "Insurance Benefits," and "Other Compensation," had been lined out. The final paragraph was one long sentence attesting that the party of the second part had read the contract and agreed to abide by its covenants as well as by any which hereinafter may be appended through said party's signature to the Ship's Articles (SS *Aurora Victorious*) and any consequent modifications thereof unilaterally effected by the party of the first part. Beneath that were Rossi's scrawled signature and the date.

Later that day, Raiford showed the Rossi file to his partner, Julie. She finished reading the contract and looked up at her father. "What he signed was no better than a blank form!"

Raiford nodded. "He must have been so happy to get the job that he didn't care what he signed."

"Or had no choice."

The contract, like the notification of death, gave both father and daughter a sense of a legal and moral emptiness as large as the ocean itself into which a man could disappear and no one be held accountable.

"I think this is one we want to handle, Julie."

"Do you want the shipping company or the underwriters?"

Raiford glanced at his watch. "Underwriters. But first thing in the morning: East Coast offices are closed now."

At 1:04 P.M. the following day, Julie's telephone rang. The marine operator said she had the SS *Aurora Victorious* on the line as requested, and then she asked whether Touchstone Agency wished to complete the call at this time. Julie said yes.

Wherever the oil tanker was, it took a two-second delay for the British voice to bounce off a satellite in reply to her query: "That's right, Miss Campbell. I'm the ship's master. Captain Boggs. If you have questions about Third Mate Rossi's death, direct them to our home office, Hercules Maritime. I have nothing to say about it."

"We received notice of his death from Hercules Maritime, Captain. But it didn't go into detail. Naturally, his mother and father would like to know as much as possible about the loss of their son. Can you tell me how it happened?"

"Died at sea. Buried there."

And apparently didn't make much of a ripple. "Was it illness or an accident? Did he suffer? Did he have any last words for his parents?"

"No time for words. Fell down a ladder, fractured his skull."

"What about a funeral service, Captain? Can you tell me something about that? Perhaps give me some map coordinates, so his parents at least know where his body is?"

"No. The hour here is late. Talk to Hercules Maritime and their attorneys, Miss Campbell. Good-bye."

Julie stared at the silent telephone for a long moment. There could be several reasons the good captain would hide behind the shipping company lawyers, none of which boded well for the Rossi family and their quest.

At three thirty-seven, Raiford received a telephone call from the Herberling Investigation Agency and Mr. Bertram Herberling himself. The Touchstone Agency's earlier inquiry to Marine Carriers Worldwide Insurance Corporation about a death on one of the Hercules Maritime vessels they insured, the *Aurora Victorious*, had been forwarded to him for investigation. Could Mr. Raiford answer a few questions?

"Your client told me this morning that they underwrite only vessels and cargo and have no liability for the crew. Why are you now interested in a crew member, Mr. Herberling?"

"The person you spoke with didn't know that Hercules Maritime has placed a claim with Marine Carriers for another of its vessels, the *Golden Dawn*. It was recently lost in the Indian Ocean—an oil-bulk-ore carrier."

Raiford thought that over. "You're looking for a pattern of negligence by the shipping company or incompetence by the crews?"

The voice held a shrug. "If proven, it could be grounds for the underwriters to negate a percentage, or even all, of the owners' claim for the *Golden Dawn*, yes."

A ship's insurance was based on—among other factors—the age and most recent inspection of the vessel's hull and operating machinery, the certification and safety records of a ship's officers, and the ability and training of its crew in standard operating procedures. Any misrepresentation could invalidate an insurance award. "How much indemnity for the lost ship?"

"Hull, cargo, and anticipated freight: five and a half million dollars, give or take the odd penny."

Raiford whistled silently: that would make anyone's petty cash drawer jingle merrily.

Herberling anticipated his next question. "Should your case develop anything that contributes to a . . . favorable outcome for Marine Carriers, I'm authorized to offer a reward for such information." He added, "It could be a tidy sum."

Tidy sums were very nice and brought a smile to Raiford's face. "I think we can work together, Mr. Herberling." He told him what little they had in their case notes.

"Thank you. By the way, I admired Touchstone Agency's work on the Medusa Investment case."

That had been a ponzi scheme promising a thirty percent return on East European investments and aimed at professional athletes who had a lot of money and little business sense. "Did you have a client in that?"

"No. I read about it in the *Paris International*. I look forward to working with you."

The next morning as Julie unlocked the office, the telephone rang. Detective Sergeant Kirby of the New York City Police Department was anxious to talk with a representative of Touchstone Agency. "I understand you people are investigating the death of a sailor on an oil tanker?"

Julie wondered if the Rossi death had been posted on the Times Square news board. "That's right."

"And that you and a Mr. Herberling talked about it yesterday evening?"

Evening in New York; afternoon in Denver. "My partner did, yes."

"Did they talk about the *Golden Dawn*?"

"Why do you want to know, Sergeant?"

The vaguely East Coast accent sharpened with authority. "Official police inquiry. What did he tell you about the *Golden Dawn* or the Hercules Maritime Shipping Company?"

Julie's atennae felt a quiver of suspicion. She had never heard a cop outside of television shows use the phrase "official police inquiry." "What precinct are you with, Sergeant?"

"What's that?"

"Your precinct and badge number. Some kind of identification."

"Identification? Sure—Precinct Fifty-Two. Badge number nine-five-six-zero-three. Now all I'm asking, see, is for a little help here—just tell me what Herberling talked about. We do it over the phone, it saves everybody a little time. No summonses, no depositions, none of that crap. Just trying to make life a little easier, okay?"

"You're calling from precinct headquarters?"

"Sure."

"I'll call you back in five minutes."

"Hey—talk to me now. I'm really in a hurry—"

It took the full five minutes for Julie to go through information in New York and finally ring the Fifty-Second Precinct. The heavy Bronx accent said they did not have a detective sergeant by that name, but they did have a patrol sergeant named Kirby. Did Julie want to talk to him?

"Yes, please."

"Then call back Monday. He's on leave."

As she hung up, her father came into Julie's office, papers in hand. "What's the matter?"

As she told him about the call, he stared out the window toward the distant mountains glimpsed between the towering new apartments, condos, and offices of Denver's burgeoning LoDo neighborhood. "Yesterday, a call from Herberling. Today from a fake cop."

"Maybe Rossi's death is more important than we know."

Raiford held out the papers. "Funny you should say that. This fax just came in from the Marine Advisory Exchange."

Page one was a receipt from the MAE for payment rendered. The other pages were what Touchstone Agency had rendered for. Page two, directed toward shippers, gave the founding date of the Hercules Maritime Shipping Company; the address and telex number of the home office in London; the type of vessels available for charter—tankers, oil-bulk-ore carriers, grain carriers—and the types of contracts the company offered: voyage or time, crewed or bare boat. The brokerage company that drummed up customers for Hercules Maritime was V. G. Braithwaite, the Baltic Exchange, London. A paragraph evaluating Hercules Maritime's performance revealed that in the past five years, shippers had filed nine civil complaints against the company, ranging from goods damaged in transport to delayed or lost cargo. Hercules Maritime had been ordered to pay four of the claims and its reliability rating had recently slipped to "Acceptable."

"That's Lloyd's lowest category. *100A, A, Restricted A,* and *Acceptable.*"

"Which is why Herberling is interested in Rossi's death."

Raiford nodded. "Customer satisfaction is almost as important as safety records for insurance rates. Add Rossi's death and that could up the insurance cost on every ship Hercules owns."

Page three held a terse history of Rossi's ship, the oil tanker SS *Aurora Victorious*: VLCC class of 334,000 tons deadweight, keel laid by Mitsui Shipbuilders on 12 Feb 88. Launched 1 Aug 89. Delivered 7 Dec 90 as the *Texaco Pearl*. Sold 2003 to Hibbard and Sons, renamed *Daniel K. Ludwig*. Sold to Hercules Maritime 2008, renamed *Aurora Victorious*. Last safety survey, April of current year, resulting in a hull suitable for seagoing service. Insurance underwriters: Marine Carriers Worldwide. A final entry held the vessel's technical description—its dimensions, capacities, and rated speed, all of which added up to just what its VLCC class stated: a very large crude carrier.

Julie tapped the sheets together. "This ship's almost thirty years old."

Raiford nodded. Most tankers in service averaged about half that. "The owners are squeezing all they can out of her."

"Yeah. This reads like a Better Business report on a shady used-car dealer: nothing proven, but buyer beware."

The following morning, while Raiford was going through the notes and documents once more, Julie tried to reach Bertram Herberling. He hadn't answered when she had tried earlier, and this time was no different: the line clicked to a recorded message asking that the caller leave a message. She finally dialed a different number, expecting a similar result. But she was surprised by a human voice, "Ahern Investigations. Percy Ahern speaking."

"Percy—this is Julie Campbell in Denver."

"Julie! The dream of my heart! When are you going to quit working for that slave-driving father of yours and join me in the most fabulous city in the world?"

"Business must be fabulously slow if you're in your office."

"Naw—I'm catching up on accounts, is all. So much

income, so little time to count it. This is, I hope, a social call?"

"No." Julie told him about Rossi, Herberling, and the non-existent Detective Sergeant Kirby. "We haven't been able to reach Herberling yet, and I'm not sure if you can do anything for us, Perse. But it's your turf and I thought I'd call. Any thoughts or suggestions? Is Herberling reliable?"

"Herberling's okay. I worked with him and his partner a couple years ago on a maritime insurance scam. What's his partner's name . . . ? Mack—that's it: Stanley Mack. And Herb gave a talk at an association meeting last year on security for port facilities. Your cop, I don't know about, but I agree it smells. It's pretty obvious somebody wants to know what Herberling told you."

That was what Julie and Raiford thought, too. "Any idea why Herberling would be interested in Rossi's death?"

"Just what he told you: looking for any pattern of faulty maintenance or poor seamanship that would reduce the insurance award on that other boat. Let me see if I can locate him—I'll try to get back to you soon. Billable time or courtesy?"

"Billable, for a change."

"Then I'll definitely get back to you soon."

Raiford moved from computer to telephone. Rossi's first ship, the MV *Helena Georgiou*, had been listed in an online shipping directory as a combination break-bulk and containerized cargo liner with a rated speed of 18.2 knots and deadweight of 14,439 tons. Owned and operated by the Langerfield Lines of Baltimore, it was of Panamanian registry and made scheduled calls at ports between Rio de Janeiro and the east coast of the United States south of Cape Hatteras. It was due to berth in Savannah, Georgia, at 22:00 hours 2 October, pier 3. Communication was via radiotelephone and short wave. No telex, no e-mail.

The radiotelephone operator put Raiford through to a woman who answered, "Bridge, *Helena Georgiou*, First Officer Steinfurth speaking."

He explained who he was and what he wanted.

"Rossi? Died at sea? Sorry to hear that." The woman may have been more sincere than Captain Boggs, but she sounded equally unsurprised. Seafaring was one of the world's most dangerous occupations.

"Did he correspond with you or any friends aboard ship?"

"Not with me. I wouldn't know about any friends in the crew. Not likely, is my guess."

"Why's that?"

"Hands sign on and off at every port. And most don't speak English."

"He was a hand? Not an officer?"

"He was a rating. Made able seaman a few months before leaving ship. Came on as seaman apprentice—a deckhand—and moved up fast. He was a hard worker and a quick learner. But he was not an officer."

"He was a third officer when he died."

A long pause. "Well, he left ship over a year ago. In Jacksonville. Maybe he took the exam after leaving."

"Is it usual for an able seaman to move to another ship as a third officer?"

"Hell no. Not on a union ship. Officers start out as cadets. Go to the maritime academy for four years like I did, or come in through the Naval Reserve. Even if he did pass the exam, he'd have had to serve as a cadet aboard a ship before he could make third. And he was not a cadet on the *Helena Georgiou*."

"So his promotion was unusual?"

Officer Steinfurth hesitated. "Officers' certifications can be bought. But if the insurance underwriter finds out about it, you can kiss your coverage good-bye."

"I'd appreciate your asking if anyone in the crew knew Rossi—and have that person call me collect. His ship owners won't provide any information about his death."

"What company's that?"

"Hercules Maritime. Rossi was on one of their tankers—a VLCC."

"I've heard of Hercules Maritime. I wouldn't work for them."

"Why?"

"Purser runs their vessels. They buy secondhand ships, hire at minimum wage or less. When the rust bucket starts to cost more than she can make, they have a fire in the hold." A snort. "And I've heard they don't look too closely at certifications. Which could be the way Rossi did it."

"They lost a ship a few months ago. The *Golden Dawn*."

"Was she one of theirs? I'm not surprised. You ought to query the Seafarers International Union, then. If Rossi was a member, they'll have an investigation into his death. If he really was a third mate, he probably joined the MMP—the Masters, Mates, and Pilots Union."

"Will you please call if you hear of anything else that might help? Collect, of course."

"Sure."

He was logging in the operator's statement of time and charges when the telephone rang again. But it wasn't First Officer Steinfurth calling back.

"Raiford—Ahern here. I was hoping your lovely Amazon of a daughter would answer. What have you two stepped in, my lad?"

"Your wife will tell you that you're too old for my lovely Amazon, Perse. And what do you mean 'stepped in'?"

"Bert Herberling. I'm in the office of one of New York's finest who would very much like to become better acquainted with you."

"A policeman? Why?"

"A homicide detective. Somebody killed Herberling."

Raiford grunted as he pressed the bar of the weight machine. Beside him, her red Stanford sweat suit streaked dark, Julie bench-pressed her own weight—148 pounds—with a long, steady inhale. Across the gym, a woman in Lycra walked rapidly on a Nordic machine, electric blue legs and arms swinging with the quick rhythm of her bronze-colored ponytail. Friday afternoons were scheduled for heavy workouts, but this time Raiford's mind was only half concentrated on his reps. He let the weights thud heavily, his eyes resting on the electric blue movement. But his mind wasn't where his eyes gazed.

"What exercise are you contemplating now?"

Julie's voice brought his thoughts back to the present, and he grinned. "Aesthetic appreciation only."

Patting a towel at her face and neck, she studied the woman. "Her hair's the same shade as mom's was."

"Yeah."

"I sometimes glimpse women who remind me of her in some way."

He nodded and pushed hard at the weight machine.

There were times when they could talk of her mother, when they would share memories of her humor, her wisdom, and those family stories and quirks of character that defined her uniqueness. But there were also other times, Julie knew, when a sudden memory could become a sharp pang. Those moments were the isolating ones—the ones that defined loneliness.

"It's been a long time, Dad."

Raiford understood his daughter's meaning and shook his head. "It would be hard to find what we lost, Julie."

"Mom wouldn't want you to be lonely."

"Being alone isn't being lonely, sweetheart. Perhaps in time . . ." He shrugged.

Which closed that topic almost before it was opened. Julie sighed and turned to the day's events. "There has to be some kind of tie, Dad."

Between Herberling's death and Rossi's. His daughter's mind worked like his own. He nodded as much at that idea as at her comment. The only explanation for the telephone call from the phony cop—possibly Herberling's murderer him-self—was that he was trying to discover what his victim might have told Julie. But though it was a mantra they had chanted over and over, it hadn't led to much enlightenment.

"Well, we know Rossi wasn't a member of any American seafarers' union." His name had not been listed in the Masters, Mates, and Pilots roster, nor in that of the National Maritime Union. In fact, the representative of the NMU had very curtly told Raiford that a high rate of deaths and accidents was to be expected when owners refused to hire experienced union labor.

"When I talked to Mrs. Rossi this afternoon, she told me they had no idea he was studying to become a ship's officer. They had been very surprised when he moved to the *Aurora*," she added. "In fact, they didn't even know he'd left the *Helena Georgiou* until he called and told them about his promotion and the new ship."

It was Raiford's turn to sigh: time to come clean with Julie. Despite her mental agility, she did not like surprises, especially any that held the odor of subterfuge. Neither, Raiford admitted to himself, did he. But the idea and opportunity had come too quickly to discuss it with her, and both had been busy on the telephones. "While you were talking with Mrs. Rossi, I had a call from Herberling's partner, Stanley Mack. He's taken over Herberling's investigation of Hercules Maritime. He told me that the electronics officer on the *Aurora* is due for leave, and that its insurance requires a replacement for him while the ship's under way."

"So?"

"So electronics officers are hard to recruit because VLCCs spend so much time at sea. And a two-week replacement is harder because it doesn't pay much."

"So?"

"So for short stints they often hire people who might not know much about seamanship but who know electronics."

"So?"

"So . . . I told Mack about my background in electronics and computer science. He says he has a good chance to put me aboard the *Aurora* as a supernumerary."

"You told me you hate ships!"

"It's only two weeks."

"You said they're too cramped for a man your size. They make you claustrophobic."

"Two weeks. And Mack's pretty upset about his partner's death, partner. He's sure Marine Carriers will go along with it. They want to pursue the *Golden Dawn* investigation."

"But you would be alone, Dad—no backup, right? And no way off that ship if there's trouble, right?"

The cardinal rule of undercover work was to always have a backup and to always have a way out. "It's expenses and two thousand a week plus the supernumerary pay," said Raiford, adding, "And Mack is also offering a five percent contingency fee on the *Golden Dawn* claim if I find anything that he can use in court. That claim, Julie? Remember? Five million dollars?"

She thought about five million dollars.

"Five percent is two hundred and fifty thousand."

That was the sum her math had reached, too. "Two weeks?"

"Two weeks' paid vacation: adventure on the bounding main, the romance of the sea!"

"You want two weeks of romance on a boat with sailors bounding on the main?"

"Well, no, that's not what—"

"How do the New York cops feel about Mack poking his nose into a murder?"

Raiford shrugged. "They're going with the theory that Herberling was killed in the course of a robbery. His wallet and watch were missing; the petty cash box was empty; the desk drawers, safe, and files were rifled."

"Mack doesn't buy that theory?"

"He says his partner would have handed over his wallet, watch, and anything else the gunman asked for, including the file on the *Golden Dawn*—which was pretty messed up, by the way. Herberling was a firm believer that things can be replaced but lives can't."

"A messy file and a willing attitude don't add up to much. Why does he think the death has anything to do with the *Golden Dawn*?"

"He thinks the wallet and watch were taken to throw the cops off. Says Herberling liked to carry his cash in his side pocket—where it was found—and his credit cards haven't been used. A robber would have cleaned all his pockets and cashed out as many cards as fast as he could. Plus, the only case Herberling was on was the *Golden Dawn*. Finally, there was that call from the fake cop asking what Herberling told us."

"Where's the *Aurora Victorious* now?"

"In the Gulf."

"Well, Florida's not too far . . ." Something in his expression warned her. "Which gulf?"

"Persian."

"Dad, that's halfway around the world!"

"I can bring you back some exotic gifts."

"I can get exotic on East Colfax Avenue."

"Two weeks, Julie. And it could mean a lot of money."

IV

Including the layover in Frankfort, the Lufthansa flight from Denver to Qatar took twenty hours. Even in the business class seats that Raiford's long legs demanded, he was cramped and restless. Between meals and movies, his mind drifted in and out of sleep, back and forth from the meeting with Stanley Mack at JFK Airport to that last quiet evening with Julie.

Despite their attempts to be upbeat and businesslike, the farewell dinner at Barolo's had been subdued. Though they both accepted the dangers of investigating people who did not want to be noticed, their talk kept drifting from the items she would cover in his absence to silences that hinted at the risks Raiford could face. The appeal of danger, Raiford had once told his daughter, was one of the reasons for creating

Touchstone Agency. It had brought him out of a dark period in his life.

Five years ago, Raiford had found his thoughts still dominated by memories of his dead wife as he stared at the snowy mountains beyond the window. The contract he was supposed to be drafting lay on his desk, and the feeling that he was deeply tired of practicing law, tired of paperwork, tired of doing what he had been doing while his wife gradually weakened and finally died in sedated numbness from pain, emanated from it. So tired, in fact, that he had been careless in drafting the contract and his client had suffered damages. Raiford had been given his choice of retiring from practice or being fired and embarrassing himself and, more importantly, the firm. He quit and spent a month immersing himself in search of some work that might take his mind off the past and focus his days and thoughts on the present. What he found took him back to his interest before law school: electronics and their use in industrial security. The Touchstone Agency was born and Raiford's new career brought him back to life. In time, it also offered focus for his daughter, whose marriage and newspaper job had both failed in the turbulent collapse of the economy.

This sea adventure, however, was a new and large step— isolating Raiford among potential enemies—and despite efforts at lightheartedness as Raiford and Julie dined, their conversation kept turning to the murder of Bert Herberling and to grim stories told by other detectives who had lost friends.

No such sentiment had pervaded Raiford's meeting with Herberling's partner, Stanley Mack. "I've told the chief executive of Marine Carriers what we want to do, Mr. Raiford. He does not want any ties between you and Marine." Mack, a short, nondescript man with thinning mousy hair, asked, "You all right with that?"

Raiford assured Mack that was the case.

"Okay. There's nothing unusual in undercover work aboard ship. In fact, a lot of owners hire a spy among the officers to report back on how a captain runs their vessel. So don't be surprised if people are a bit suspicious of you. You'll be a fifteen-day replacement for the electronics officer, a third mate by the name of Reginald Pierce." He laid out papers to be signed. "Here's your contract."

Some paperwork that was only slightly shifty, a crimp—a recruiting agent—who, surprise, surprise, was willing to take an extra fee for a discreet service, and Raiford became the temporary employee of convenience. The first contract authorized a hefty percentage of Raiford's pay to be deducted from his first, and only, paycheck for something called Insurance and Personnel Investment Costs. The second was almost identical with the one signed by Rossi, except that none of the paragraphs had been lined out. Apparently, electronics personnel rated more TLC than the navigation ranks. Raiford was named supernumerary with a rank equivalent to third officer (Electronics), and appointed on a fifteen-day contract.

Mack explained that Raiford would not be required to sign the Ship's Articles; cadets and supernumeraries were excused from that ritual because of the special nature of their duties. The Ship's Articles, which superseded a seaman's general contract, only applied to regular hands. They spelled out what a crewman's workload would be, the watches he would stand, the deductions for clothing, special services, and commissary items to be drawn from his pay. The use of Ship's Articles was, Mack told Raiford, the standard way crews of convenience were hired, and was necessary because each ship had differing requirements and offered differing amenities. It also saved time in labor negotiations since a sailor could not sign the Articles until he was aboard ship— and usually under way and out of sight of land. The term "shanghai" wasn't used, Mack said, but the result could be the same.

"It all depends on how much freedom the owners give the shipmaster to deal with his personnel, and how willing the master is to give benefits to his crew."

"What about the master of the *Aurora Victorious*?"

"Boggs? I haven't heard much about him. The directory lists his master's ticket as awarded by the Pacific and Orient line in 1990. He's generally qualified for any type and all sizes of vessels, with additional qualifications to command vessels that haul hazardous cargo."

"That's good?"

"Oh, yeah. P&O's a well-established fleet. Old-time. They don't give anyone command unless they think he's thoroughly qualified."

"But Boggs left them."

"It may not have been his choice. In the nineties, a lot of companies reduced their fleets and cut back on their long-term charters. My guess is Boggs, being junior, lost his ship in that reduction." He explained, "A big tanker's going to cost around thirty thousand dollars a day just sitting there, so you don't want them idle. Many oil companies own about sixty percent of what sea transport they might need at full capacity. When oil demand drops below that sixty percent, companies sell off part of their fleets—usually the older vessels—and lay off crews. When it picks up, they hire from independent fleets until they decide whether to build and crew their own new vessels. In really hard times like the last few years, even the independent fleets like P&O cut back on vessels." Mack added, "If that's what happened, Boggs was probably damned happy to find any ship, even one owned by Hercules Maritime."

"Did Rossi sign a contract with his recruiter, too?"

"Probably. And from what you tell me, the crimp probably set him up with his mate's ticket, as well. For an additional wad of cash, of course."

"Any way I can find out who Rossi's crimp was?"

"Without his recruiting contract, it'll be hard. Every port in the world has crimps." Mack frowned. "Any idea where he boarded the *Aurora*?"

"His parents thought it was the Gulf of Mexico."

"That might be something—VLCCs can't call at many ports. I'll see what I can find out."

"I'd like you to send copies of everything Herberling had on Hercules Maritime to my daughter, Julie Campbell. She's covering the office for me while I'm gone: the *Golden Dawn* files, the *Aurora Victorious*—whatever. And the name of Herberling's contact at Marine Carriers."

Making a note in a small black book, Mack said, "I'll FedEx it today."

He then gave Raiford a list of the officers on the *Aurora Victorious*, as well as the ship's schedule, its primary means of communication—e-mail, fax, and Inmarsat—and the Ocean Region Codes and Ship ID number, promising to include the same information in the packet to Julie. "If you need to use the ship's radio, here's the frequency for Marine Carriers Worldwide. They monitor twenty-four/seven, but call only if necessary."

"Cell phones don't work?"

"Depends on where you are. Close to shore, they may. Offshore, probably not." After a pause, Mack added, "If you get in trouble, it could take as much as forty-eight hours to fly someone out to you." He leaned back on the hard black plastic of the lobby seat and studied Raiford's face. "Don't forget what happened to Bert. He was a good man."

Raiford nodded. "I'll try to find out if there's any connection."

"You're going to be pretty much on your own."

That had been his daughter's comment, too, and he answered it the same way. "I've been there before."

If Raiford was going to be on his own, it would not be at busy Doha International Airport. Signs in English and Arabic advertised Marriott, Sheraton, Hertz, Alamo, and other familiar names and welcomed English-speaking travelers to the "Gateway to the Arabian Gulf." Proof of a visa, crew status, and sufficient funds cleared him through immigration. A turbaned Sikh held a card with his name. With a "Welcome, sahib," he carried Raiford's bags to a Mercedes-Benz taxi. The temperature, Raiford read, was 40°C and humidity was at 24.1 percent. But the abstract numbers did not prepare him for the impact of the heat. Blinking against the glare, he settled into the air-conditioned taxi as it swung through the busy streets and past the soaring modern office towers of Doha into a countryside of flat, almost treeless sand and rock. To the nasal wails of Middle East music from a CD, the taxi lurched down a strip of glaring, heat-shimmered concrete. Some 40 kilometers later, instead of following the highway toward the commercial port of Mesaieed, the vehicle angled onto a bumpy tarmac road. "Landing boat come here—closer to ship." A cluster of flat-roofed, concrete block buildings huddled under the sun. Beyond them stretched the silver gleam of the Persian Gulf. The national flag, maroon with a serrated white band, drooped on a flagpole.

A guard wearing a checkered headdress and carrying an automatic weapon—it looked suspiciously like an Uzi—read over Raiford's letter of appointment and studied his passport photograph. Then, expressionless, he raised the gate, let the taxi pull to the front of one of the squat buildings, and disappeared back into his air-conditioned sentry box.

The driver lifted Raiford's two canvas suitcases from the trunk. "Please to wait here for boat," he said and held out a chit to be signed and a hand to be filled. As the taxi's diesel engine pinged up mottled sand and wind-scoured rock, Raiford began to feel isolated.

The sun pressed on his head and shoulders, but the sense of real heat came from the close, woolly air. It withered his nose and throat into scratchy flesh, and he could feel sweat running like ants down his back and under his arms. From the sand, additional pulses of heat rose up through his shoes to make him shift from one burning foot to the other.

"Here, mate—come inside before you're toast." A bony splinter of man wearing a brightly flowered shirt opened the door of a long, almost windowless building and leaned out into the glare. "You're the new man for the *Aurora Victorious*, right? I've called her for you. The launch'll be here in a bit."

Raiford breathed with relief in the air-conditioned half-light of the large, barrackslike room.

"Bleedin' hot, 'specially if you ain't used to it. And this is the beginning of the cool season. This here's the landing lounge—welcome to use it whenever you come through. No whiskey, though. Arabs don't like it. Have to bring your own, and a lot of them likes that well enough. Been aboard the *Victorious* before?"

"No." Raiford looked around the stark room with its low ceiling and gritty concrete floor spotted with old stains. A vacant bar held empty stools and a television set chattering in Arabic. Four men sat in beat-up lounge chairs reading or smoking and sipping coffee. They glanced at him without expression before turning back to their silence. Near a computer bearing a sign reading "2US$ per kilobyte," a smeary chalkboard listed a dozen ships' names followed by dates. Among them was the *Aurora Victorious*, and the dates for yesterday and today. "They part of the *Victorious*'s crew?" asked Raiford.

"No, a BP tanker. Contracts are up and they're being repatted. Waiting for their bus to Doha. Yank, are you? What's your rating?"

"Third mate. Electronics."

"Ah—tech-o. Given how big you are, I'd've thought you were navigation. Alec's the name—everybody calls me Lexie. I'm the landing manager. Something cold to drink?" He limped toward the bar. "There's the list chalked up. Prices are in dollars and Qatari riyals. But we'll take any hard currency. Daily exchange rates are over there." He pointed at a second television screen that scrolled silently through the world's currencies measured against the dollar, the yen, the pound, the euro, and the riyal.

The constantly moving numbers focused an odd feeling for Raiford: despite the solidity of the large and ugly room, it had a quality of impermanence. The barren sand and rock, the waiting men, and his own disorientation gave a sense of being in the aura of something just out of sight, something vast and fluid and continuously changing. It was a something that had created this mirage of installation and humanity. Served by the building, the armed guard, the gabbling manager, the men waiting in silence, that vague something became embodied in the numbers on the screen. And it did not distinguish between the humans and the buildings and the equipment that served it. They were equally interchangeable, equally replaceable. And Raiford was now one of those numbers.

Lexie talked as if he hadn't spoken to anyone for a month—and perhaps he hadn't. Not in English, anyway. "Not many come ashore at the landing here—mostly supernumerary arrivals and departures like yourself. Not a damn thing to do and even less to see. Tankers aren't tied up long enough for a proper shore leave, so mostly the crews stay aboard and work or sleep. This lot, they don't speak English—Pakistani, I think they are. Most of the bloody crews anymore are our little brown brothers. Can't speak English worth a damn. Rossi? Third mate? Never met him, as I know of. Tankers come and go, sometime two or three a day, and like I say, who in his right mind wants to set foot here? Though some of 'em get a little crazy being on ship all the time and they'll take even this place for a change of scenery. It's an okay place if you like sand—underfoot, in your clothes, in your teeth. Sand and wind, wind and sand, and mind you the heat never leaves even at night. *Golden Dawn*? Never heard of her, and if she's a small one she wouldn't come here anyway. What part of the States you from? Colorado? Never been there. Florida, once—Jacksonville. Norfolk, New Orleans, Baltimore. Ports of call, you know. I was in the black gang, back when ships had a black gang. The *Victorious*? Two or three times a year she ties up, which ain't bad for a tub as old as she is. Another drink? Right you are—can't get enough liquids, can you? Tell you, confidential-like, she ain't a happy ship. Tough on her crew. Hard work, long hours, and low pay. Every time I see a hand get repatted from her, they're glad to go. Don't mean you, of course. You'll get treated right as an officer and a white man should. Repatted? Repatriated—paid off and sent home. Works her hands hard, her master does, and the first mate's a regular bulldog, they say."

When two Chinese wearing dark blue coveralls and oil-stained canvas shoes carried Raiford's suitcases out of the lounge, Lexie followed, still talking. The crewmen led Raiford down the narrow pier to a small launch. Under its bleached canvas awning, an officer in a glaringly white uniform with narrow epaulets welcomed him in basic English: "Mr. Raiford? I am Third Officer Suk Wan Li. You come please, we go ship." A clatter of Chinese ordered the hands to stow the luggage.

With a quiver of noisy engines, the boat settled its stern as it cut through the still water. The huddled buildings of the landing, the pier, the mottled shore vanished into heat haze as the minutes passed. Raiford stared across the iridescent streaks and boils of passing oil slicks. Gradually, out of the blur of horizon, a long, low streak emerged. At one end of the streak, a gleaming island of white superstructure rose. A single stack, squat and straight, trailed a lazy brown smudge to one side. As the tanker grew nearer, he could make out heavy ropes holding her blunt bow to a large float. Bright orange hoses rose out of the water to stubby booms amidships. Beyond and perched on a low smear, a few small, boxy buildings and a complex of silver-painted pipes and valves were mirrored in the sea. The launch slowed; the massive rust-streaked black-and-red steel wall towered like a cliff. An accommodation ladder, tiny against the gigantic hull, dangled down to a platform just above the water. Although Raiford had a vague understanding of the behemoth's dimensions, he could not help asking, "How big is that thing?"

"Three hundred fifty-four meters in length. Fifty-eight meters at beam. Twenty meters draft. Three hundred twenty-six deadweight tons maximum load—maybe more than two million barrels. Twenty nine thousand horsepower." The answers were chanted like a familiar chorus by the white-jacketed officer.

Raiford translated the figures roughly into feet: just over eleven hundred feet long, two hundred feet wide, and—when loaded—sixty plus feet below the water's surface. Another class, the ultra large crude carrier (ULCC), was even bigger. But at a fifth of a mile long, the *Victorious* was colossal enough, and he understood why his would be the first question of any newcomer.

One of the sailors grappled the platform with a boat hook; the other hopped out to tie the launch to a cleat. High above, up the long spidery-looking ladder, a tiny human stared down, its face shadowed by the white dot of an officer's cap.

"Captain Boggs," said the third officer. "He waits. You go quick."

V

Julie's computer displayed "1 New Message." Time stamped 6:03 A.M., it read "R. aboard AV. Mack," and a FedEx package from the same source arrived just after noon. Julie glanced through the thick file of documents and placed a call to New York. "Have you heard any more from my father?"

"Nothing since his e-mail from the shore facility," said Mack. "We probably won't hear much. Not until he has something to report and a chance to do it." His voice warmed a bit. "He's probably lounging around the ship's swimming pool, drinking beer."

She smiled at that thought. "He said you promised him a vacation cruise."

"I'm sure that's what it will be."

She hoped so. Her dad had operated undercover a lot more

than she had. On this job, however, he was violating the procedures, as she had reminded him. Granted, they went where the job called, and they both agreed that people shouldn't get into this business unless they were willing to take chances. But *chance* had a matter of degree, and that degree should always be minimized. This time, it had not been.

She focused on the Herberling documents as a means of shoving away nagging thoughts.

The *Golden Dawn* file opened with a black-and-white photograph of the ship at sea. Six hatches ran from its stubby bow to the rear island. Outside the hatches and tucked inside the ship's rails were pipes for oil. Three short masts, one at the bow and two behind the third hatch, provided cargo-handling booms. A longer pair of booms folded inboard between the sixth hatch and the ship's island. A raked smokestack rose above the topmost bridge—the navigation level—whose open wings protruded as far as the sides of the ship below. An accompanying page described a single-screw, diesel-powered motor ship of 40,377 tons deadweight, built in 1979 to carry ore, bulk freight, or oil; speed rated at 15.5 knots.

The history of the ship's last voyage listed its owners—Hercules Maritime—and flag—Cyprus. Departed Fremantle, Australia, 17:00 (GMT) 6 November, last year; cargo, bauxite; destination, Abu Dhabi, Arab Emirates. Master, Capt. Kenneth Minkey. She dropped her pilot at 17:56 off Rottnest Island. Made routine Telex reports to the Hercules home office at noon (local time) over the following eight days. Average sailing speed: 14 knots. At 11:53 (GMT) 15 November, she reported that she was in heavy seas and her cargo had shifted. At 14:40 a severe list to starboard brought water through number three hatch. At 17:54 water entered the fuel bunkers. The engines failed at 18:17. That was the last transmission. At 06:00 (GMT) 16 November, Hercules Maritime notified Marine Carriers Worldwide underwriters and asked all ships in that area of the Indian Ocean to report any sighting of the MV *Golden Dawn*. At 12:00 (GMT) Hercules Maritime called for a search. No contact with vessel or survivors. Assumed lost with all hands. Location of last transmission: Long. 83' 21" east, Lat. 9'14" south. Claim for lost vessel and cargo filed Friday, 23 November.

Last was an abstract of the underwriter's report. The ship's documents as well as harbor and port authorities had noted several problems with the vessel: the condition of the ship's pumps (low p.s.i.), the thickness of the plating on the starboard bow encompassing holds one and two (corroded and pitted sections), and the presence of hairline cracks in the forward collision bulkhead. She underwent repairs at the Malacca Dry-dock and Shipyards, Singapore. An invoice and diagrams detailed the hull samples and repairs, and a stamped document from a certified marine inspector in Singapore verified the repairs. A Marine Carriers Worldwide agent, Dorothy Fleenor, declared the vessel insurable on February 10, and coverage was issued beginning 00:01 (GMT) 11 February, last year. A final page in differing type noted that the bodies of two oriental males wearing life vests bearing the name *Golden Dawn* had been picked up at sea on 21 December by the MV

Dirk Pitt at longitude 97'08" east, latitude 11'22" south. No identification. Buried at sea.

Julie placed a call to Marine Carriers Worldwide and asked for Mrs. Fleenor.

"Yes, I was the agent on that transaction." Her voice was cautious.

Julie explained her connection to Herberling and the Rossi case.

"I don't understand what that death has to do with the *Golden Dawn* claim."

"It's hypothetical," Julie admitted. "But Mr. Herberling was asking about the Rossi incident just before he was killed, and I'm picking up the pieces of his investigation. Can you tell me what kind of insurance the *Golden Dawn* had?"

"Let me pull it up." It took a minute or two, then the woman's voice came back to tell Julie that the cargo insurance was for one voyage, which wasn't too unusual because single-voyage was the cheapest policy. However, and this was aberrant, the hull was insured against total loss.

"Why is that unusual?"

"Most owners limit the liability to a partial value of the hull to lower costs. Since this policy had no deduction from the hull's value, its rate was appreciably higher." In fact, Mrs. Fleenor admitted, the coverage came to nine hundred US dollars a day. "But the *Golden Dawn* had recent dry-dock repairs and passed her safety survey, or we wouldn't have insured her."

"Then why pay for full coverage?"

A brief silence. "It does seem contradictory."

A contradiction like that would raise questions in Herberling's mind just as it did in Julie's. And should have in Mrs. Fleenor's.

The ship also had coverage on its anticipated freight. "If, for any reason, the cargo was not ready on time for shipping," Mrs. Fleenor explained, "or could not be shipped in that vessel, the owners could file claim for the loss of that piece of business."

"How much?"

"Seven hundred thousand US dollars."

"They'll collect?"

"The ship was unavailable, so, yes, that claim should be honored."

"Unless Mr. Herberling found evidence of insurance fraud?"

"That would negate any and all payments, of course. But as far as I know, nothing like that has been found."

"But the owners could earn a great deal of money if their ship sank."

Her reply was less an answer than a slightly defensive explanation. "One of the challenges of maritime insurance is to balance sufficient coverage against making a loss enticing for an owner." Her voice dropped. "It's possible that balance may have been missed on this one."

Julie did not ask who was first in line for blame if that were so. "Has Hercules Maritime made other claims for lost ships?"

"Not with us. Their insurance record in general is satisfactory. It's one of the principal factors we consider before issuing a policy."

"Mrs. Fleenor, did Mr. Herberling have grounds for suspicion?"

When the woman finally answered, it was with resignation. "Yes. Looking at the configuration of that policy now, I'm afraid so."

"But at the time, you recommended insuring the vessel."

"I . . . yes. It was a bad time for me personally. . . . Perhaps I wasn't . . . Yes."

Julie waited, but the woman added no more. "How might I find out who insured the crew?"

"Mr. Joseph Wood at Hercules Maritime. You could ask him."

"I've tried to reach him. I haven't had any luck."

Another pause. "Maybe he's too busy to reply. They have a small office and staff. Most tramp companies do." Then, "You might try their broker in London—Braithwaite, I think. He might know who they used as recruiters for the *Golden Dawn*, and certainly the recruiter's contract would detail any insurance for crew members."

"Thank you, Mrs. Fleenor."

Julie had her doubts about the sincerity of the woman's "You're welcome." She had dumped a lot of worry on a person whose only consolation seemed to be that she wasn't the first insurance agent to make a bad call.

The final section of Mack's package was Herberling's case notes. Scraps of paper had been photocopied onto a

41

single sheet. They showed a quick, nervous scrawl in half-completed phrases that indicated Herberling's thoughts. One heavily wrinkled fold of envelope listed five names and addresses headed by the initials "A.V." The first name was familiar: Boggs. Four more names—Bowman, Pierce, Shockley, and Pressler—and accompanying addresses followed. The addresses were all in England. Pierce was the man her father was replacing. Assuming the other names were still aboard the *Aurora Victorious*, Julie could ask Mack who they were.

Circles around the first three names could mean either a completed inquiry or a need for more detail. Another scrawl threw some light on a possible reason for Herberling's interest: "crew certification??" Under that was Raiford's name and telephone number and the phrase, "Rossi death—*Aurora Victorious*??" But nothing showed a clear connection between any of the names and the lost *Golden Dawn*.

Other notes indicated other directions the dead man was considering. "Herc. Record safety violations/safety histories," "financial history—current status," "crew interviews." Julie figured that Herberling had been hunting what any detective looked for first: the money. It was also apparent that he had not settled on a single direction, unless some papers were missing.

Following in Herberling's footsteps depressed Julie. The notes gave a glimpse into the dead man's mind, and his investigative procedure was not all that different from her own. She could step in with little adjustment. But it brought the murdered man as close as an old, and now lost, acquaintance, and reminded her where her father was.

Reformatting the information into her computer, she outlined possible approaches. She also added two headings not in the original file: "Fake Detective Kirby" and "Herberling's murder."

VI

Boat wasn't the word for the *Aurora Victorious*. Even *ship* seemed too small. Raiford had read the figures describing the vessel, but he had not fully imagined it.

There were no cramped passageways filled with conduits, banks of control wheels, gauges, and some maniac screaming "Dive! Dive! Dive!" Instead, the ship's corridors were wide with carpeting laid down to prevent sparks and covered with a temporary canvas runner for protection against oil stains during loading. All was eerily silent. A plastic plate on the wall at the base of a stairway, also wide and carpeted, told Raiford that he was on the middle bridge deck. The door of his quarters opened to a short entry that led past a shower and toilet on one side and folding closet doors on the other to arrive at his so-called cabin. It was like a hotel that charged too much and used decor to make you think you were getting your money's worth: fully carpeted, windows framed in drapes, air-conditioned, furnished with wood-laminated pieces showing wear from a lot of predecessors and constant cleaning.

A small writing desk with two brass lamps, a worktable hinged to the wall, a couple of dull yellow sofa chairs with a veneer coffee table between them, and—below the square plateglass windows—a sofa bed. King size, he had been told, because officers, spending all but thirty days a year at sea, sometimes brought their wives along for part of a voyage.

Even the two windows were not the little claustrophobic circles he had assumed they would be. They looked out over the broad deck that stretched ahead for a thousand feet. The wide surface—painted a dull, dark green—held the low bulges of hatches and inspection plates, spurs of upright stand pipes, port and starboard hose and cargo derricks, and, halfway down the deck, a cluster of pipes, valves, loading arms, and short ladders that made up the loading and discharge manifold. That was where the oil lading hoses were connected. The manifold crossed from port to starboard over steel tubes that ran like a spine from the ship's island to the bow. In the distance, the vast flukes of an anchor and spare screw shimmered brassily. Almost out of sight near the distant number one fire hydrant platform, a couple of bicycles used by crewmen to traverse the deck lay on the sun-scorched steel. Beyond that, the curved black line of the vessel's bow lifted into the band of silver heat-haze that masked the horizon.

Unlike the navigation officers, Raiford was not assigned a watch. The most junior navigation officer, Suk Wan Li, had the third watch, the eight to twelve, which finished at noon and at midnight. It gave the Chinese officer his choice of either sleeping through breakfast and being hungry while on his first watch, or rushing through it before going on duty. Next senior, Second Officer Norman Shockley, had the four to eight, with a late breakfast and a warmed-over but leisurely dinner. First Officer Pressler took the first watch—the twelve to four and midnight to four—with all his meals properly served. Captain Boggs did not have an assigned watch; he appeared on the bridge periodically to check his junior officers when they were at sea, and he worked twenty-four to forty-eight hours at a stretch when the ship was loading or passing through dangerous waters. Otherwise, as Raiford discovered, the captain was seldom seen except occasionally at coffee in the wardroom after supper. Pressler, as first mate, ran the ship's routine navigation operations.

Raiford's official duty schedule, his contract said, was from eight A.M. to five P.M., five days a week. It was the same schedule as the four engineering officers who relied on the automatic controls to run the ship at nights and during weekends. Except for the fact that the underwriters demanded a full complement of engineering officers for a vessel to be insurable, the turbines probably could have run on automatic for the rest of the time as well. That fact wasn't lost on the younger engineering officers, the second and third mates, who viewed Raiford and his computers as their replacement in some not-too-distant future. They did not welcome that idea or the man who represented it.

A phrase in Raiford's contract stated that the supernumerary would be on call twenty-four hours a day while the vessel was under way. Captain Boggs, who interviewed Raiford in the ship's office underneath the ship's flag and drinking coffee from a ship's mug, asked if Raiford clearly understood what those ship's words, *on call*, meant.

"It means I can't go anywhere off the boat, right?"

Boggs leaned back in the squeaking desk chair and stared hard at the big man. "You bloody well don't know much about seafaring, do you, Mr. Raiford?"

He answered cheerfully. "Not much, Captain. My job's the electronics, and they're the same ashore or asea."

"Yah—computers!" Boggs poured himself another mug of coffee from the glass bulb steaming on its small hot plate at the corner of his desk. "This is a ship, not a boat." In the metal ceiling over his head, a slotted vent fluttered a small strip of cloth to show that the ventilation system was working, and a faint pattern of grime fanning away from the grill showed that it seldom stopped. The odor of oil tainted the cooled air. "Well, electronics is your job and your only job. You stick to your work and keep the hell out of the way of the ship's company—officers and ratings both. Hear me?"

"Suits me." And it was pretty clear that it made no difference to the captain if it did or did not suit Raiford. "Care to point me toward the operations guides and manuals? I'd like to get checked out in the programs and hardware."

The bloodshot and slightly bulging eyes stared from beneath a single ledge of wiry gray eyebrows. "The first mate'll show you around. Mr. Pressler. He's up on the bridge deck. Follow me—we'll see what he makes of you."

Despite his rounded shoulders, the captain was almost as tall as Raiford, but only half the weight. With a roll that swung his torso from side to side, he led up the central flight of stairs covered by a temporary canvas runner scuffed with oil stains. At the top of the stairway, he pushed through the polished brass of a wide door onto the navigation bridge. The enclosed wheelhouse, also air-conditioned but smelling more strongly of oil, ran the full width of the island and, at each end, heavy weather doors led to open wings that protruded out over the sea almost a hundred feet below. In the center of the bridge, unmanned, a tall ship's wheel stood before the dome of a compass. But that was almost the only nautical touch. The rest of the decor consisted of banks of monitoring lights for the engine room and loading control room; control stations for various machines and their readouts; indicator panels for collision avoidance, navigation, and the sea depth measured port and starboard as well as fore and aft. Other panels monitored and controlled docking and maneuvering, on- and off-ship communications, and even personnel administration. Raiford had a glimpse of what his daily routine would consist of: checking and rechecking the reliability of the hundreds of sensors and connections and the miles of wiring that fed information to the processor units on the bridge and to the loading and engine control rooms below. Each major panel had its own Teletype machine for a written record of activity by the computers; and a variety of toggle switches, buttons, and dials allowed operators to interrupt the programs in case of emergency. It could have been the control console of a large and complex airliner.

The bridge's only occupant peered tensely through wide sheets of scratched Plexiglas down at the green deck. Beyond the ship's rails, a level sea looked dwarfed and harmless. As the bridge door clicked shut, the stocky figure muttered, "Ham-handed little barstids! Call themselves goddamn sailors!"

"Mr. Pressler."

"Sir!" The man did not turn from what he watched. Raiford noted the heavy muscle of a sun-scorched neck that disappeared into a white linen jacket taut and unwrinkled across broad shoulders. A hand seemed to have pressed on a once tall man to mash his body thick and wide.

"Here's Mr. Raiford. He's our supernumerary for Mr. Pierce."

Irritably, the man turned to look and then rocked back to take in Raiford's height. His expression shifted from irritation to a coldness verging on enmity. Raiford had seen it before in men whose sense of self was suddenly dwarfed by his size.

"Mr. Raiford, is it?"

"Call me James."

"I'll call you any goddamned thing I please. Is that clear?"

Raiford's eyelids drooped in that sleepy look that masked the flash of anger in his eyes. "Clear."

The captain gave a little hissing noise that seemed to be a laugh. "Mr. Raiford is new to the sea, Mr. Pressler. A supernumerary, remember. We'll have to make some allowances for his lack of shipboard manners."

"A goddamned landlubber. Is that the best they can send us now?"

"He's qualified in electronics, our Mr. Raiford is. That's what his papers say, anyway. I leave him in your hands, Mr. Pressler. Acquaint him with the bridge controls." Another hissing laugh and the door clicked behind the captain's rolling lurch.

"See that!" Pressler's thick finger jabbed toward the deck below. "Bloody sodding slant-eyed yellow barstids can't handle a fucking hose coupler without spilling a dozen barrels of goddamn crude!"

Raiford leaned toward the Plexiglas that radiated heat from the outside air. Far below at the manifold halfway down the expanse of dull green, three tiny figures in dark overalls wrestled frantically at the stubby boom that lifted a stiffly awkward orange hose more than three feet in diameter over the ship's side. Around their feet and among the lateral pipes that twisted to join the long central spine of tubes spread a widening pool of foamy, chocolate brown liquid. Pressler grabbed a microphone, his voice bouncing back in a metallic echo from a loudspeaker somewhere below, "Hose that goddamn deck right now, you bleeding spastics—get water on that now! Chop chop!"

The speaker popped off and he said as much to himself as

to Raiford, "Sand all over the goddamn deck and they start spilling crude. All we need's a fucking explosion."

"Sand? Out here?"

"Blown aboard from the desert, Mr. Raiford. The desert's made of sand, in case you didn't notice. One spark from a grain of sand in that hot oil on that hot metal deck and you can bend over and kiss your arse good-bye." He looked quickly at Raiford's feet. "And take off your street shoes, you stupid lubber. Don't you know enough to wear plimsoles when we're loading tanks?"

"Plimsoles?"

"Rubber-soled shoes—sneakers—tennis shoes—whatever the hell you goddamn Yanks call them. Take those off, damn your eyes—we're loading. No leather shoes worn when we're loading! Absolutely no smoking aboard when we're loading. Off—now!"

Under his stocking feet, Raiford felt a quiver in the canvas that temporarily covered the wheelhouse deck. "I suppose the evening barbie's called off too?"

"The—!" Pressler wheeled about to stare up at Raiford for a long moment, jaw slack. Then he threw his head back in a guffaw. "The evening barbie! Haw!" From anger to laughter as if some switch had suddenly changed his mood. "The evening barbie! By God—!" He slammed his palm against the painted steel ledge inside the windows and shouted another laugh at the overhead. "Come along, Mr. Landlubber. I'll have the steward give you the Cook's tour of our floating goddamned barbecue!"

VII

Through the window of the banking airplane, Julie made out familiar landmarks in the dusk: the tapering spike of the Empire State Building, the Chrysler Building's graceful silver thrust, the obsidian box of what used to be the TWA Building with its heliport on the flat roof, and, near that building's foot, the domed grayness of Grand Central Station. And the sudden emptiness where the World Trade Towers once stood.

Then they leveled off to glide over a marshland already dim with twilight and clotted with white specks of resting birds. Ponds and rivulets flickered red from the setting sun, then, with a blur of concrete and a solid thump of touching wheels, the engines began to reverse. The brakes launched her against the seat belt with an impetus that carried her impatiently through the covered ramp and toward the faces waiting to meet friends and family. At the back edge of the small crowd, a balding man of medium height and anonymous appearance, wearing an equally inconspicuous tie, caught her eye with subtle question.

"Stanley Mack?"

"A pleasure to meet you, Miss Campbell." His eyes, slightly bloodshot, glanced up her tall figure and then to her hand. "Any luggage?"

"Just what I'm carrying."

"Good. They're waiting for us."

They were the representatives of Marine Carriers World-wide, who had urged Julie, as the representative of Touch-stone Agency, to fly to New York for consultation. The only name Julie recognized was Mrs. Fleenor's. Her face and voice betrayed a lot of strain as she stood to shake hands. The two other representatives at the conference table were men in their fifties or early sixties who were able to mask their anxiety with some success—their careers weren't at stake. "It's a lot of money, Miss Campbell. Not that Marine Carriers World-wide cannot guarantee its policies, of course. But you must understand that we have to be very aggressive in defending ourselves against any and all false claims."

The one who spoke like a lawyer was in fact the company's senior attorney, Herbert Ferguson. He spent the first ten minutes making the point that bona fide losses were one thing, but that insurance fraud was something else. It hurt the whole shipping industry, drove up policy costs, and if successful, established an unsavory precedent that might entice other owners to attempt fraud. Consequently, every claim had to be thoroughly investigated and malefactors prosecuted to the fullest extent of the law. The idea wasn't new to Julie, and she felt a touch of dismay as it dawned on her that Ferguson's pep talk might be the real purpose of the long flight to New York. The man was worried that Touchstone Agency would not take the *Golden Dawn* case as seriously as Marine Carriers wanted them to. And perhaps that a woman might not be able to do the work that a man could.

Mr. Mohler, the company vice president overseeing casualty assessment, nodded in agreement. Fortunately, he didn't have much to add.

Mack nodded also, and murmured a time or two that he was certain Miss Campbell understood the seriousness of the issue, that the Touchstone Agency has a sterling reputation, and that he—Mack—would still be the supervisory investigator. But Ferguson listened to himself more than he listened to Mack.

Mrs. Fleenor kept her attention on the papers in front of her.

Julie listened and watched.

Finally, Mr. Ferguson stated that it was an immense pleasure to have met Miss Campbell, that he was gratified to have this opportunity to air the concerns of Marine Carriers Worldwide, and that he had every confidence that she would do her utmost to bring the issue to a speedy and satisfactory conclusion. He didn't add "or else," but the firm handshake and tight-jawed, challenging smile made that clear. Mr. Mohler nodded and shook hands just as firmly and then they were gone.

After a brief silence, Mack, embarrassed, said, "He wanted to meet you in person. Like he says, it's a lot of money."

Julie had run across the type. They swarmed at the lower levels of senior executives, anxious to prove to those under them that they deserved to be where they were, and to those over them that they deserved to be promoted. "Is Mr. Mohler your boss, Mrs. Fleenor?"

She had pale blond hair that might have been dyed to hide early gray. It was bobbed in a fashion that accentuated rather than softened the length of her bony jaw. Thick glasses perched on her narrow nose and made her violet eyes look large and blurry. If she ever smiled, she might have had a wide mouth; right now it was pursed with worry. "Yes."

"Did he authorize issuance of the policy on the *Golden Dawn*?"

"His signature is required, yes."

"But you do the real work and he usually goes along with your findings?"

A faint smile acknowledged how often a male fool was placed above a woman with talent. Then she shrugged. "Until now."

Mack asked, "Does he blame you for the claim, Dorothy?"

"He hasn't said it in so many words."

Julie watched the woman's long fingers slide absently across the small stack of papers in front of her. "Have you found out any more about Hercules Maritime or the *Golden Dawn*, Mrs. Fleenor?"

"I've managed to speak with some sales representatives in

other insurance firms, people I've met over the years. But I'm not sure how much they can help."

"Have they told you anything at all?"

"No one I spoke with has had any trouble with Hercules Maritime. I did find out that about five years ago they filed a claim with Coleman and Thorstein on the loss of a medium-sized tanker, seventy thousand tons, the SS *Indian Flyer*. Apparently she broke apart in heavy seas off northern Spain. The cause was determined to be structural deterioration, and the claim was paid. The person I spoke with said there was no finding of culpability against the crew."

Mack added, "Most hull insurance covers negligence of master, officers, crew, or pilots, since human error's the cause of most accidents."

"Does that clause apply to the *Golden Dawn*?"

Mrs. Fleenor replied. "It does. Unless there's willful culpability by owners or operators. That is, if the operators did something to cause the *Golden Dawn* to sink, or refused assistance that might have saved the ship, then all or a portion of the insurance would be voided. We don't know anything about that, since all hands on the *Golden Dawn* were lost. But if the owners knowingly employed operators with a record of unsafe practices or who were not properly certified for their position, then willful culpability can be charged against them by the insurer—by us." Her fingers traced across the manila folder. "From what you tell me, Miss Campbell, Mr. Herberling's thoughts had been in that direction. I understand he had been looking into any pattern of carelessness by Hercules Maritime in hiring officers for their other ships?"

She nodded. "It looks that way. And, please, both of you call me Julie."

"Julie—" She wasn't comfortable with first names. "Well, that suspicion does not seem to fit the loss of the *Golden Dawn*. The vessel was old, and I discovered that one of her sister ships had also broken apart not too long before."

"Was the sister ship owned by Hercules, too?"

"No. Another independent. But I didn't ask who. I can call back if you want me to."

Mack answered that one. "Not unless we need it, Dorothy."

"I hope you don't mind, Miss . . . Julie . . . but I telephoned Mr. Wood in London and told him you had been trying very hard to get in touch with him and would probably be calling soon. He said he would be available to you." Her fingers caressed the stack of papers again. "I assumed you still wanted to speak with him."

"You assumed right, Dorothy. How did you manage to get through to him?"

For the first time her voice showed a quiver of emotion, but Julie wasn't sure if it was victory or anger or an escape of tension. "Marine Carriers Worldwide hasn't yet paid his claim. He's very eager to hear from us." She added, "I—ah—did not mention the *Aurora Victorious*. I only told him you wanted to ask a few questions about the *Golden Dawn*. I allowed him to believe that you were working in our office."

"That was wise, Dorothy."

She slid the papers tentatively across the table toward Julie. "I couldn't remember exactly what I sent you, so much of this is duplication. I want to be certain you have everything I do."

The only new document was a photocopy of the complete insurance policy. Julie thanked the woman and placed the photocopy in her folder, not because she wanted it, but because it seemed to make Mrs. Fleenor feel better.

The ride down in the elevator with Mack and Mrs. Fleenor was long and silent. When the two detectives, free of the woman and her muted anxiety, were finally on the street and weaving through sidewalks crowded with stiff, anonymous faces, Mack said what Julie felt. "If the company has to pay the full claim, Dorothy's going to be the sacrificial lamb."

"And if I can show that Hercules Maritime is at fault, she keeps her job?"

"That's it."

"Know anything about her?"

"Just what's in the security file: lives over in Jersey, clean police record, clean credit record, divorced, two kids, one handicapped in some way. I think the other's in college now, but I'm not sure. No hint of question about her." He glanced at Julie. "Why?"

"She indicated earlier that she had some personal problems that might have clouded her judgment about issuing insurance on the *Golden Dawn*."

"Problems? What kind?"

"She wasn't specific. A hint . . . more of an explanation to herself, it seemed."

Mack frowned. "She's been with the company a long time. No hint of dishonesty or ineptitude . . ."

"Maybe Marine Carriers would be better off firing Ferguson and keeping her."

"Yeah. Listen, I'm sorry about that, Julie. When he asked to have you come here, I thought it was for something important. I should have known he just wanted to hear himself talk."

"At least it opened the door for me to go see Wood."

"See him?"

Julie nodded. "Our clients want me to go to London and make some noise about their son."

The home office of Hercules Maritime Shipping Co. was a couple of blocks from the Tower Hill Station. Julie came out of the Underground both aware of and saddened by armed police scanning the crowds of passengers. Standing by a kiosk for a few seconds, she got her bearings. A torrent of traffic dotted with glossy red double-decker buses sped just beyond the concrete steps leading down from the Underground entrance. Across Tower Hill Road, parked tour buses nosed one behind the other at the foot of the mottled gray and white walls of the Tower of London. The gothic piers of Tower Bridge and its elevated metal crosswalk rose beyond the Tower's curved whitestone caps. The smell of fried fish and the flutter of souvenir pennants marked street hawkers. At the head of a queue of tourists snaking beside the Tower's dry moat of clipped lawn, stood the flash of a Beefeater's red and gold splendor. Mixed with the familiarity of the scene was a remembered touch of excitement dating from the time of her first visit to England for her junior year abroad at London University, and the stir of those bittersweet memories made her forget the reason for this trip momentarily.

But those memories were of events well past, and her path now led away from the crowds that surged toward the Tower's tourist centers, pulsing with the beep of the pedestrian lights. More than one man in the passing crowd glanced at her face and figure, and a few leaned toward her in the attempt to snag her eyes with their own. She remembered the sexual aggressiveness, but this time she understood that those male hormones were their problem not hers. She strode briskly down America Square where the sidewalks, at least, were relatively empty. A turn onto Crosswall Street pinched off the traffic noise. Number 17 was an isolated door flanked on one side by an Indian restaurant and on the other by a stationer's shop. A steep, narrow stairway smelling of wood rot and lit by one dangling bulb led to a small landing with two doors. One was closed and bore no nameplate. The other hung half open to show a none-too-clean toilet and sink crammed into an unlit cubicle. Julie, being a detective, tried the knob of the closed door.

If the rule of thumb for staffing the headquarters of a tramp company was "one ship at sea, one man in the office," then Julie figured Hercules Maritime had about ten vessels. The large room wasn't designed for walk-in traffic; two rows of desks took up almost all the floor space, and the muffled chatter of telephones, telexes, and fax machines made an unceasing noise like distant surf. A large world map sheeted over with acetate half filled one wall and bore smears of partially erased grease pencil. Rosters of ship's names and ports were stuck on bulletin boards that filled space between large windows looking across a narrow gray emptiness at other office windows. Dots of colored pins signaled meaning to those who could read their code. Shirtsleeved men moved between the computers at their desks and the maps and charts on the walls, adjusting pins, erasing or noting comments, pulling worn reference texts from a long bookshelf and thumbing rapidly through the pages. The idea of the display boards, Julie figured, was that anyone could see at a glance the current location and status of every ship owned by Hercules Maritime, as well as the offers of freight from the brokers dealing with the world's commerce. The intent young man at the desk nearest the door finally looked up from the pattern of colors on his computer screen. "Something you want here, miss?"

"I have an appointment with Mr. Wood."

His neatly trimmed head bobbed with surprise. "There." A shirtsleeved arm jabbed toward one of three doors at the back of the busy room and darted back to his keyboard.

Julie read the thumbtacked business card and knocked. A voice said, "Come."

Mr. Wood did not look up from rattling the keys of his computer. On a stand in the corner of the tiny room, a printer buzzed through a tray of paper. Finally, the man raised his head, surprise lifting his heavy eyebrows. "Yes?"

Julie introduced herself. The man's dark eyes blinked once and he wagged a finger at the single chair beside the desk before finishing his typing. He pushed ENTER and the printer again started buzzing. "Mrs. Fleenor said you would be telephoning." He leaned back to gaze coldly at Julie. "From the States."

"I happened to be in the neighborhood. And you've been difficult to reach."

"I am a very busy man, miss. Especially at this time of day." He nodded at the in-tray full of papers. "Ship's status reports, brokerage offers, chandlers' bids, fuel quotes, all of which came in last night from around the globe. All to be attended to before the quotations change. I understand you have questions about the *Golden Dawn*? I have one for you: it has been almost a year, why hasn't Marine Carriers honored our claim?"

She did not correct his assumption that Marine Carriers employed her. "Such things take time, Mr. Wood." Julie guessed that Wood was in his late thirties, but the man's dark hair and olive skin didn't show age. And his taut expression didn't give away much, either.

"I trust that means there will be no problem with the claim. It is part of my collateral for obtaining a replacement vessel."

"No real problems, I'm sure. But a few questions do need to be cleared up before the issue is closed."

"Oh? Well, Miss—ah—the issue seems quite defined to

me. Your company insured the vessel, the vessel was lost at sea, and now the indemnity is due. What questions might there be about that?"

Julie opened her leather folder and thumbed through an impressively thick sheaf of papers, most of which were blank. "Let's start with the type of coverage you chose for the *Golden Dawn*—insurance against future cargo, single-voyage hull insurance, no deductible. That latter seems a bit out of the ordinary for a routine voyage, doesn't it?"

"Really? I always understood that the purpose of insurance was indemnity against the extraordinary. That proved to be the case, didn't it? And remember, please, that your own agent drafted the policy and that we paid what you asked in that additional—and expensive—no-deductible coverage."

"Have you had any further information about the vessel?"

"You would have been promptly notified if we had."

"Of course." Julie shuffled a few more pages. "A second point concerns the weather recorded in the *Golden Dawn*'s area on the day she disappeared. Satellite pictures for the entire twenty-four hours show no cloud cover at those coordinates, and no log entries from ships in the vicinity reported bad weather." Julie stared down at the blank sheet. "Yet the cargo was said to have shifted because of heavy seas."

"Squalls and high seas of a very local nature are not uncommon anywhere at sea, miss. As any man with any seafaring experience knows. And in that part of the Indian Ocean, the currents and configurations of the sea bottom tend to make the waves eccentric, as do occasional earthquakes. Remember the tsunami in Indonesia? No cloud cover that day, either. Now, it is remotely possible that the bauxite was initially loaded in such a way that even a mildly rough sea could shift the cargo. But our policy clearly covers against loss caused by negligence of master, officers, or crew, as well as perils of the sea. So the vessel was covered under either contingency."

But willful misconduct by the crew was not. As both of them knew and as Julie's silence stated.

"I would also remind you, miss: all hands went down with the ship, as the two bodies that were found almost a month later clearly indicate."

And, as Mack said, that ended the investigation into willful misconduct by the crew. "You've had a recent death aboard another of your ships, haven't you? The *Aurora Victorious*?"

The man's eyebrows pinched together in a dark frown. "We lose several crewmen a year to accidents usually caused by their own carelessness. Seafaring is one of the world's most dangerous occupations."

"Can you tell me anything about Third Mate Rossi's death? Exactly how and when it happened?"

"Is that in the slightest way pertinent to our *Golden Dawn* claim?"

"Not directly, no. But it may be pertinent to Marine Carriers's evaluation of its other policies with Hercules Maritime."

Wood pushed back in his chair. Its spring twanged shrilly. "That sounds as if it's a threat."

"Only a request for information, Mr. Wood. The information itself may or may not turn out to be threatening."

Without taking his angry eyes from Julie's, Wood pressed a switch on his intercom. "Mr. Goff—please bring in any information we have on a recent death aboard the *Aurora Victorious*. I believe it was a third mate." He folded his hands on the desk, eyes still on the young woman who had entered his office to coolly imply that he was lying. "My concern is with the management of our vessels. I am not concerned with their crews."

"Is Mr. Goff the person the *Aurora Victorious* reports to?"

"For all routine matters, yes."

A tap and the door opened. A young balding man with a full beard glanced at Julie. "Excuse me, miss." He leaned across her to place a manila folder on the desk. "We have only these telexes in the file, Mr. Wood."

"Thank you, Robert."

As the clerk left, Wood glanced over the two pages and then handed them to Julie. The first read, "Third Mate (Nav.) Harold Rossi died following fall down ladder way." The final line gave the time and date of transmission, and Julie noted them: 17 May, 17:33 hours (GMT). The second message requested computation of Rossi's pay and allowances less deductions, asked that the replacement be flown out to the ship when it neared Cape Town, and noted that Rossi was buried at sea 14:00 hours (local time) 18 May. Julie noted that, too; it was something she could give to Rossi's parents. "No medical diagnosis?"

"Only the Japanese routinely have doctors aboard their tankers. However, according to the traditions of the sea, every first mate on all our vessels—including the *Aurora Victori-ous*—is trained in emergency medical techniques to render first aid. Additionally, company policy is for the shipmaster to locate the nearest vessel with a doctor aboard and, if neces-sary, to rendezvous with it for medical assistance. Air evacu-ation by helicopter is another option if the vessel is within flight range of a major airport and if the injury is of sufficient seriousness. This humane policy could lead to considerable expense, miss, since a tanker the size of the *Aurora Victorious* costs more than two hundred thousand of your dollars a day at sea. But it is our policy, nonetheless." The shoulders of the man's pinstriped suit rose and fell. "However, if a hand dies, there is little any doctor can do."

And much time and money saved. "Can you give me the ship's location when Rossi was buried?"

Wood made it obvious that he was mastering his impa-tience as he pressed the intercom button again. "Mr. Goff, please give me the coordinates of the *Aurora Victorious* on"—he glanced at the date line on the telex—"May 18, 14:00 hours local time."

"Directly, sir."

A minute or two later the intercom gave a timid peep. "Sir, at that date and time, the *Aurora Victorious* was approxi-mately fifty-one degrees east, eighteen degrees south. That would be some three hundred miles due east of Madagascar and approximately one hundred miles west of the Mauritius and Rodrigues Islands." A pause. "Seems a bit off course for the usual Gulf to Cape Town route, doesn't it, sir?"

"Thank you, Mr. Goff." Wood took a deep breath. "Anything else before you go, Miss ah—?"

He did not stand to see her out. "Please tell your employers that I consider your line of questioning to have verged on insult, that their delay in settling our legitimate claim is both arbitrary and unwarranted, and that I will reassess my future needs for underwriting in light of their performance in this affair closely. If their delay should cause Hercules Maritime any material loss whatsoever, a legal suit will be forthcoming. Good day."

Julie smiled. "Thank you for your time, Mr. Wood."

VIII

By late afternoon, lading would cease and the *Aurora Victorious* would hose down and stow in order to get under way. Pressler summoned the chief steward to the bridge. Short, Taiwanese, and in a white jacket, he never seemed to tire of smiling. "Johnny, this mountain of flesh here is our new electronics bloke while Mr. Pierce is on leave. Name's Mr. Raiford—a supernumerary. He don't know a goddamned thing about ships and even less about shipboard manners. You show him around. Get his head screwed on right."

"Yessah—please this way, Mr. Raifah."

Because of lading, Raiford's tour was limited to the aft of the vessel. Johnny, smiling, warned him that no smoking was allowed anywhere aboard while they were at a terminal. "Okay at sea to smoke in own cabin or in wardroom only."

"Don't smoke at all—bad for the health."

"Ha, yes. Very bad: go boom! Ha ha ha."

They began with the navigation bridge, an open deck capped by the mast and, at the top of that, the radar scanner. Five enclosed bridge decks rose to form the island some forty feet above the main deck. Below the main deck, in the bowels of the hull, were at least five more levels.

The deck just below the navigation bridge, where the first mate prowled, was the captain's bridge. Raiford had already glimpsed Captain Boggs's roomy quarters on the starboard side. Johnny told him that Chief Engineer Bowman had a similar suite on the port side. Between, and taking up the remaining space of that entire span, was an owner's suite that was seldom used. "Owner never comes aboard. Good thing—big cabin to clean." Outside and across a walkway aft from those suites was the swimming pool tucked at the base of the towering smokestack. "Too hot to use now. Too hot to look at, too. Better when we get under way."

Next came the upper bridge deck. It held the senior officers' quarters. The four or five doors were spaced along a wide corridor that had the strip of temporary runner to protect the forest green carpet from oily plimsoles. The middle bridge deck held the junior officers' cabins, including Raiford's and Third Officer Suk Wan Li's, along with those of four petty officers. "Steward for this deck is Wang Wei—English call 'Woody.' Anything for your cabin, you ask him." An even wider, gold-sparked smile. "My cabin right here—petty officers' cabins. Wang Wei is very good steward or he has much trouble with me." The lower bridge deck, just above the main deck, was one of the ship's principal social centers. It contained the movie theater, library, and infirmary, as well as the officers' games room and dining saloon with its adjoining wardroom. "You spend plenty time here, Mr. Raifah." Johnny glanced around the carefully ordered wardroom with the eye of a professional caretaker. The dominant colors were a restful dark green and cream. Thick drapes flanked the large windows that looked forward to the bow. "Drapes must be shut every night. Hard for lookout on bridge to see if light comes out at night."

Leatherette sofas, deeply cushioned armchairs, and a scattering of coffee tables were placed at one side of the club-like space. The other side held a wet bar with half a dozen stools and a long shelf full of bottles in a variety of languages. Mounted around the room were a television set, a stereo, shelves holding rows of worn paperback books, a shortwave radio with an attached radiotelephone console and mounted instructions for its cost, times of operation, and use. There were no company flags or emblems on display in this room. "Whiskey price is very good. Very cheap."

The crew's entertainment area was below on the main deck—a combined games room and mess hall that ran the width of the ship. Its smaller windows, lacking drapes, looked aft to the stack housing and the fantail beyond. This one, too, had a television—large screen—and stereo sets, but the decor was more functional and easier to clean. Just below the main deck were the crew's quarters. One-

and two-man rooms lined a promenade of green asphalt tiles. It ran down both port and starboard sides of the hull and was lit by a band of twin portholes outboard, looking over the sea. Inboard, each room had a large square window that brought in light from those outboard portholes. Through them bunks, desks, washbasins, and padded chairs could be glimpsed. It was, Raiford thought, a long way from a ratty hammock, a hunk of hardtack, and a cat-o'-nine-tails.

"Did you know Third Officer Rossi, Johnny?"

"Yes, sah. Very bad he died." Then, "You know him too?"

"I met his mother and father. They asked me to see if I could find anything of his they could have to remember him by. He was buried at sea, right?"

"Yes, sah. Buried at sea."

"Did you clean out his room when he died? Gather up his things?"

"Officer do that, sah."

"Do you know what they did with his stuff?"

"You ask officer about Mr. Rossi, sah."

That was the answer to all other questions about Rossi: ask one of the officers.

Below the crew's space were the decks and rooms that would be Raiford's chief interest as electronics specialist: the operating panels for the engines, the communications center, the housing room for the navigational equipment and its related computers, the loading control room for the storage tanks. Clean and efficient, the sterile and fluorescent-lit space reminded him of any slightly outdated computer center ashore. Although he was continually bending his neck to pass under steel door frames, he was relieved to find plenty of headspace everywhere except in the engine room. There, his claustrophobia was stirred by the latticework of cramped ladders, railings, and platforms that made him duck and dodge. Narrow passages sliced between wheels and banks of dials and switches; speaker tubes and rows of levers reached to snag his shoulders. But for all the clutter of those manual controls, the space was void of life. It was as if here, in its heart, the ship was its own master and a human hand was both unnecessary and unwanted. It was Raiford's job to ensure the computers kept it that way.

In the loading control room, they found a man in jeans and plimsoles. His black T-shirt bore a skull and the words GRATE-FUL DEAD in silver ink. He was probably in his midthirties, but the casual dress made him seem younger. He stood tensely in front of a wall-mounted diagram dotted with red and green lights connected by varicolored lines. Beside the diagram was another panel filled with alert lights, green numbers changing regularly, control dials that he touched lightly now and then as if tuning an instrument. The man glanced at Raiford and then back quickly as a pair of red and green dots switched their colors.

"Mr. Shockley—Mr. Raifah. Temporary electronics officer, sah." He explained to Raiford, "Mr. Shockley is second mate."

"Pleased." A quick handshake whose softness went with the small paunch swelling beneath the T-shirt. He turned quickly back to the illuminated diagram that made a large and intricate pattern in the center of the flickering lights. "Served much time aboard tankers?"

"First time ever. On any ship."

"Oh?" The second mate pulled his eyes from the control board for an instant and he looked more closely at Raiford. "The owners must be getting desperate."

Raiford shrugged. "They needed someone fast and my name was on the list. Regular replacement was sick or something."

"Ah." His eyes went to Raiford's stocking feet. "Well, you'll want a proper kit. Johnny'll take you to the ship's slop chest. Mind the prices—company sets them and they're damned high, so buy only what you need." Then, "I'm second deck officer. That means I supervise the loading. First officer's duty, normally, but . . ." He ended with a lift of shoulders that said it didn't make any difference as long as the job got done. "We're a fully automated tanker. Automated navigation and steering, automated engine. Automated loading system. If something goes awry with the electronics, you'll be kept damn busy I can promise you." He spoke to Raiford, but his eyes stayed on the lights and the rows of dials labeled with pump and valve numbers and functions monitored: speed, suction pressures, quantities, ballast level, cargo level, ship's trim. "You'll be kept busy anyway, what with the maintenance and routine servicing. No pleasure cruise, this."

"The electronics give you a lot of trouble?"

"Well, she's old, the *Aurora* is. But the circuitry manages to hold up right well. Knock on wood—if you can find any. Sensors and switches are always the problem. Corrosion. Salt. That's why I keep a close eye on the loading. That's what this is, the loading control room. This computer here is the Lodicator. Tells the valve controls how to do the job. How much ballast out of which tank, how much oil into which tank, and when. Stuck valve, and everything becomes a hell of a mess. The diagrammatic tells me how well the ship's answering. Sweding machine here"—he nodded at another console— "gives a projection of the ship's stability based on the current loading pattern. These are the override switches for manual control. Ticklish time right now: getting up to ullage—full on the tanks. Load up to twenty thousand tons an hour of warm, light oil. Only twelve thousand of this stuff, though. Heavy. But the computer does it all: fills each tank to ninety-eight percent capacity, distributes the load so the ship stays trim and won't go brittle or capsize, opens and closes valves to the center cargo tanks and the wing cargo tanks in the right order. That's what these lights are on the diagrammatic—red open, green closed."

Raiford had a chilling thought. "Who programs the computers?"

"Done ashore. Computer gurus ashore figure that out. Home office sends out the software and programs we need at each port. Don't vary too much: the load's always crude oil. But we do get different types of crude—we'll be going up to Al Ju'aymah to complete loading, and that's a different weight and type. Lighter. Have to keep that separate from the Halul crude—that's one of the things that makes this part of the loading plan so ticklish. A tank of ballast beside one full of heavy crude puts a lot of shear strain on the old hull. Damn good thing the Gulf's a calm sea."

"You mean we could sink?"

"Happens. Don't want to, of course."

"Of course."

Johnny had disappeared sometime during the second mate's monologue, but Raiford stayed to watch Shockley fine-tune the pumps' speed and press a macro on a keyboard that recorded tank numbers, load, and time completed. "How many tanks does the ship have?"

"Fifteen for cargo plus a bunker for ship's fuel. Six center tanks, ten wing tanks. Full cargo capacity is 326,000 deadweight tons of crude." He looked at Raiford. "Canadian, are you?"

"American." The red and green lights flickered, numbers changed steadily, needles swung across dials or fell back as pumps adjusted to the valves, and the cargo compartments were filled in rotation to keep the ship level. Except for the steady murmur of the air conditioner and the occasional chatter of a printout from the Sweding machine, the room and the steel world surrounding it were silent.

"Have you been on the ship long?"

"Going on four years, now. Before that, was third mate on the SS *Kuwait Champion*." Shockley eyed the green numerals. "Another couple of years and I'll strike for first. Which is why I don't mind filling in for Pressler—gives me a chance to learn the job, eh?"

"That's moving up pretty fast, isn't it?"

The face tried to hide its pleasure. "Oh, I suppose. But if it can be done, why not? Who knows how long the bloody shipping industry's going to need crews? SS *Keymatic,* that's what will sail the seas before long. Got to build up my retirement while I've still got a job, right?" He laughed. "You, now, you might end up being the only soul aboard. No crew, no officers, just the bleeding electronics tech to keep the computers happy. You and that bleeding machine there"—he waved a hand at a keyboard and screen filling a metal drop leaf mounted on the bulkhead.

"That's the main computer?"

"Not the main one, no. Some kind of slave terminal. Don't know how it works. Don't want to, either. Your job, not mine. You'll be like the Ancient Mariner, eh? All alone and water, water everywhere, eh?"

"They can't sail ships without people."

"I used to think that too. Can't sail ships without a black gang. But now there's no more black gang, no more deckhands. It's just 'navigation.' Question is, how many people will they need? You realize a ship this big carries only thirty-eight men? That's full complement. Captain to mess boy— thirty-eight men. And mark my words, they'll be cutting that back soon enough."

Raiford let his silence indicate agreement. "Did you know Harold Rossi?"

In the silent room, Shockley's pale blue eyes stared at Raiford long enough that he twitched when the Sweding machine chattered out more data. "What's Rossi to you?"

"I met his parents in the States. They told me he had some bad luck."

"Bad luck, all right. Terrible what happened to him. Nice chap."

"How did he die?"

"Fell down something, I hear. Didn't see it." The pudgy face frowned at the consoles, and the faint fellowship that Raiford sensed as the two men stood together in the stark and plastic-smelling emptiness suddenly ebbed.

"Well, like I say, I didn't know him. His parents called me just before I left and asked if I'd find out a little more about how and where he died. The letter they got from the owners didn't tell them much." Raiford added, "They wanted me to send on his personal effects, too."

"I see."

Raiford watched the man. Shockley watched the gauges. The consoles took all his attention and he didn't offer any more commentary.

After a while, Raiford asked, "Do you know what might have happened to his gear?"

"No."

"His parents wanted me to ask. Sentimental reasons. You understand."

"Yes."

"Well, I'd better get unpacked."

"Right." The pale blue eyes shifted Raiford's way for a second. "You'll want to read up on the equipment manuals. Had a spot of trouble with one of the relay switches in tank five. We'll want it looked at before we reach the next loading platform."

IX

The broker who located cargo for Hercules Maritime's ships said he would meet Miss Campbell when the Baltic Ship Exchange closed at five. "Can you find my office?"

Julie had circled Mr. Braithwaite's address on her *London A to Z* map. "Shouldn't be a problem."

"Excellent. I will look for you then and there."

The circle on the map turned out to be more of a problem than she expected. Mitre Street, easy to miss, was one of those tiny avenues that bent between larger thoroughfares. It had originated, probably, as a medieval public path cut between land holdings. The address itself was tucked beyond a narrow vehicle tunnel leading to Mitre Mews. In fact, if her eye had not been caught by one of those pale blue historical markers—stating that the young journalist Charles

Dickens often lunched on this site when it held the Pickwick House and Pub—Julie might have missed the alley. But Mr. Braithwaite waited patiently in his third-floor walk-up, cigarette smoke thick in the air and ragged stacks of paper and reference books contrasting with the tables full of up-to-date electronics. Each of two desks held sleek computer screens angled toward a comfortably padded swivel chair contoured like an astronaut's. A long table against a wall held additional modems, two fax machines, telephone answerers, printers, and even something that looked suspiciously like a security scrambler and decoder. Each desk telephone had about twenty service buttons, and a telex machine filled another corner.

"Ah, you found me! I was growing a bit worried." He hopped up, youthful in movement despite the deep wrinkles of a chain smoker and hair that showed gray turning white. He had a white, clipped mustache that was fringed with nicotine and spoke of colonial service. "Bit difficult to locate, being in the mews and all, but a quiet location—delighted, Miss Campbell." He held her hand for an extra second as if feeling the warmth of her young flesh. "Delighted!"

"It's kind of you to take time to see me, Mr. Braithwaite."

"Not at all, dear girl. Not at all!" He pushed aside the book he was thumbing through—*International Shipping and Ship Building Directory*—and grabbed a dark blue blazer on a coatrack. "Let's abandon ship before the blasted telephone rings. Sun's below the yardarm here, but not in New York or San Francisco, eh?" He jabbed another long cigarette butt among others that filled his ashtray, tucked his striped tie behind a pewter button, and herded Julie out the door.

To Braithwaite, Julie was "dear girl"—possibly, she thought, because he could not remember her name. As he guided them to his favorite pub he rhapsodized about America and things American. "Love Florida, dear girl! And my cousin lives in Los Angeles. I visit quite often—travel's the prerogative of a bachelor, isn't it? And I've even been to your wonderful Colorado: the Grand Canyon. Magnificent!"

The Grand Canyon, created by the Colorado River, was in Arizona. But Julie was reluctant to correct such enthusiasm. And even if she wanted to, the man would have been difficult to interrupt. Maybe because he worked in the shipping industry, Braithwaite had caught the Ancient Mariner syndrome.

The pub—the New Roses—was a short two blocks away on Leadenhall Street, busy with afternoon traffic flowing out of the city. Etched glass, brass lamps, and dark oak. No ferns. Ashtrays on every table. Julie had a shandy, the older man a whiskey and side of water, no ice. They found a less crowded corner away from the squawk and roar of an electronic fruit machine—"Blasted things are everywhere now, even here!"— and Braithwaite lifted his glass eagerly. "Chin chin!"

Julie sipped her cool, light drink and spoke quickly while the man's mouth savored his scotch. "Have you worked with Hercules Maritime very long?"

"Oh, yes. Since they began in, I believe, 1988. They're one of our smaller clients, but steady. They've managed to stay afloat in these perilous times."

"The industry is in difficulty?"

"Very much so. Even the bulk liquid fleets. As late as 1980, the British fleet had almost fourteen hundred vessels flying the red duster. The number now is less than three hundred. All the owners are moving to flags of convenience and crews of convenience—can't afford not to. British Petroleum flagged out its entire fleet as early as 1986." He lit a cigarette, the alcohol on his breath sending a tiny plume of flame off the end of the tobacco.

"But Hercules Maritime is in good financial shape?"

"I'm not privy to their accounting books, dear girl. I deal only with their freight contracts. However, their ships are seldom idle."

"Did you arrange charter for the *Golden Dawn*?"

He nodded, pursed lips sending out a stream of smoke. "Bauxite out of Fremantle, aluminum ingots from Abu Dhabi to Seoul. I was seeking a cargo in the China Sea for her return to Fremantle when I heard of her loss. Terrible, of course—all hands. An all too familiar story, now. It's these flags of convenience, dear girl. Crews aren't trained as well as they used to be, equipment isn't surveyed as rigorously. But the sea is as unforgiving as ever."

"Accidents have increased?"

"Oh, yes! In my thirty-some years, we've had a growing number off the coast in our own waters. You're much too young to remember the *Torry Canyon* going aground in 1967. Nothing like your *Exxon Valdez*, of course—only thirty thousand tons of oil spilled. But shocking at the time and a precursor of things to come: Liberian registry. In 1970, fourteen seamen died when the *Pacific Glory* and the *Allegro* collided off the Isle of Wight—both Liberian flag tankers. A year later, another Liberian tanker, the *Amoco Cadiz*, ran aground off Brittany with a large spill. In 1987, the *Skyron*—Liberian again—and the *Hel*—Polish—collided in the Channel off Folkston. Less than two years later, the *Phillips Oklahoma* and the *Fiona*—Liberian and Maltese flags of convenience—collided and created a twenty-mile oil slick off the Humber estuary."

He wet his throat with a quick sip and started up again before Julie could slip in a question. "In 1991, the *Zulfikar*—Cypriot flag—was running in the Channel at speed without adequate radar, watches, or even lookouts, and sank a trawler. Killed six fishermen. Six months later, the trawler *Ocean Hound* went down in the Dover Straits, hit-and-run by a vessel that failed to render help or even report the collision. Most likely, it was a flag of convenience VLCC so large it didn't even know it had run over the trawler. Killed all five lads, nevertheless. Two years later, the *Braer* grounded and broke up off Shetland: eighty-five thousand tons of crude spilled. You guessed it: Liberian flag. Then the *Tharos* collided with the *Cam Sentinel* at an oil platform off Scotland. And not two years after, the *British Trent* and the *Western Winner* collided. Both flags of convenience. And you of course know what happened recently off Spain's Atlantic shore. Were any of those vessels insured by your company?"

"Not that I know of. But I wonder if—"

"Not coincidentally, vessels that fly flags of convenience usually have crews of convenience. The *British Trent*, registered in Bermuda, had British officers but a crew from Sierra Leone. The *Western Winner* was registered in Panama, officered by Koreans, and crewed by Burmese." He shook his head. "All those accidents were the result of human error, which comes when you have mixed crews who can't speak one another's languages. And poor training—or none at all. Drink up, dear girl. It's not often I have the pleasure of conversation with a lovely and intelligent young lady."

"Have you sailed on many ships?"

"Oh, no. I used to be dreadfully ill just crossing the Channel on a calm day. Thank heavens for the Chunnel. I've never boarded a vessel and have absolutely no desire to. Prefer to fly. Much quicker. Besides, I know far too much about the safety records of vessels. But damned little about aircraft. Makes me feel a bit more comfortable. Fool's paradise, eh? No, I'm no sailor. All I do is send the ships where the cargoes are."

"You handle the *Aurora Victorious* as well?"

"Certainly. Though she's currently on a time charter, so there's little call for my services until the time's up. The Arabian Gulf to the Mexican Gulf, carrying crude for BP. I think the contract lasts another sixty-five weeks. Though I'd have to glance at the charter party to be certain. Does your company need that information? Most willing to cooperate with the underwriter chaps. And I must say"—he reached to pat the back of her hand—"you're a most attractive underwriter's representative."

"Thank you. Did you hear anything about the death of their third mate?"

"Only that it occurred. Tragic, of course, but not surprising. The world's tanker fleets lose up to three hundred men a year, and climbing. Collision and explosion are the main culprits, caused by human error of course. Volatile cargo. Crews can't wear nylon shirts because static electric sparks from the cloth could set a tanker ablaze. Amazing, isn't it? And then there are the everyday casualties from slippery decks, heavy equipment, gassing—any number of clever ways a poor sailor can die."

"Gassing?"

"Hydrocarbon fumes are quite toxic, and tank inspection is one of the most dangerous undertakings in a generally dangerous occupation. Has to be done of course, but even after flushing the fumes out of a tank, bubbles of the stuff can float about. Invisible but quickly lethal. Two or three lungs full and a chap's unconscious. Three or four minutes and brain damage occurs." He added cheerfully, "Death comes after about six minutes. I've heard tanker men say they've asked their mates to let them die if they've been out for more than four minutes. Prefer death to being a vegetable, I suppose. Can't say I blame them."

"Don't they have breathing gear?"

"Certainly—Drager equipment. But there's always malfunction and human error, dear girl. Human error always, aboard ship or aboard platforms like your famous Gulf spill, eh?"

"Do you know if Hercules Maritime has other claims pending with underwriters?"

"Claims?" It took him a moment to shift tracks. "Oh—the *Golden Dawn*. No, I suppose Lloyd's would know. They're the certification society Hercules Maritime uses for their vessels. Both the *Golden Dawn* and the *Victorious* were certified by Lloyd's." He explained, "Shippers always ask for the vessel's certification society and the date of its last safety survey. These affect their insurance rates, you understand."

"You have a very good memory for dates and details, Mr. Braithwaite."

A blush made his mustache seem whiter. "Ah, no. It's my occupation, after all. And I studied Egyptian history at university—makes a chap absolutely reflexive in his use of memory, you know."

"Egyptian history?"

"Yes. So how did I become a shipping agent? Needed a job, dear girl. Would much preferred to have been a university don, but not much call for Egyptologists. However, it turned out to be good training for what I do: close and quick reading, exercise of memory with a plethora of arcane detail. Must be a bit like your work, eh? Investigations, names and dates, seemingly irrelevant details, that sort of thing?" He toasted her with his glass. "Seems a bit odd, a girl as young and attractive as you being an investigator. It's certainly no longer the world I grew up in."

"Almost as odd as an Egyptologist becoming a shipping contractor."

"Eh? Oh. Hadn't thought of it that way. I suppose you needed a job too, eh?"

"Have you spoken to other investigators about Hercules Maritime?"

"Your Mr. Herberling telephoned a fortnight ago, I think it was. Wanted what I had on the master and the officers of the *Victorious*."

Julie remembered the photocopy of the wrinkled scraps of paper that had been found in Herberling's case notes. One page had held a list of names and addresses, some circled. The other page had her father's name and that of the *Aurora Victorious*. "Were you able to tell him anything?"

"I told him what little I knew about Captain Boggs and promised to try and find information on the others. But he's never rung back. I assume the information's become irrelevant."

"Herberling was murdered last week."

"Oh, my!" After a pause, Braithwaite finished his whiskey with a gulp and gazed away at a glass panel whose etching depicted gracefully intertwined roses. "Anything to do with— I mean, ah . . ."

"We've found no connection." Nor was Braithwaite's report on Boggs found, either. "The police think it was a burglary."

"But you have your suspicions?"

"Care to tell me what you came up with on Boggs?"

"Oh, certainly. He was made redundant when BP flagged out its fleet. Spent several years waiting for another command, I hear. A not unusual story, unfortunately. Finally came to Hercules Maritime as master of a midsize tanker, the *Shining Dawn,* and moved up to the *Aurora Victorious.*"

"Any personal or professional problems? Any history of indebtedness or credit problems?"

"I really can't say. Certainly no legal issues. Owners and insurers are very particular about that sort of data, they are. As for being in debt, I suppose four or five years without work would cause hardship. Don't see how it couldn't, unless he or his wife had other income, of course." The cigarette paused just below the mustache as Braithwaite remembered something. "Which they might well have—their home is in Hampstead Heath. Rather posh area, so they must have money from somewhere."

"What about the other officers? Have you heard anything about them?"

"Not a great deal. The first mate, Pressler, has a bit of an odor about him—something about an investigation for assault or even manslaughter on one of his earlier ships. Nothing proven—not enough to keep him from getting another berth, leastwise. The chief engineering officer, Bowman, is very senior. Wouldn't be surprised if he retired in another year or two. The other officers, both navigation and engineering, all apparently have satisfactory records. They're quite young, but that's the way with so many of the new officers nowadays."

"Did Herberling ask you for any other information?"

"Only the registrar entries and home addresses for the officers and ratings on the *Aurora Victorious.* He was particularly interested in their licenses, but I found nothing out of the ordinary there. Oh, yes—he wanted any information I had on the *Aurora*'s course of travel. Couldn't help him with that, either. I know the sailing and docking dates, but I don't get daily reports like the owners do."

"You told him that?"

"Well, sent him a fax explaining that he'd have to ask Hercules Maritime. Wonderful machine, the fax. Works twenty-four hours a day and one doesn't have to waste time waiting for someone to answer one's ring. Very convenient for my line of work, you see, dealing with vastly different time zones."

Julie thought of something else. "Did you look at Third Officer Rossi's license?"

"Yes! Mr. Herberling asked particularly for that." He tapped the ash from his cigarette. "Very little there, of course. Brand-new officer and all. But I did discover he was licensed as a third officer by the Brazilian board." He added, with a shake of the head, "Now I have no chance to send that information to Mr. Herberling, do I?"

"Brazil?"

"It's not uncommon for more and more chaps to get their licenses wherever they can—crews of convenience, you see, and one country's license is respected by all others." A shrug. "Even if one nation's examination is far less rigorous than, say, in Britain or the United States."

"Could Rossi have bought his license without taking an exam?"

Braithwaite nodded. "It's possible. Difficult to prove. For

underwriting purposes, however, it would be very dangerous. Could open an owner to a charge of negligence or even abetting. It would negate the vessel's insurance. But of course you know all that."

Julie took a sip from her glass. "Did Herberling say why he wanted this information?"

"No. Seemed to have his reasons, just as you do. And I was—and am—always happy to assist the underwriters to keep insurance rates down. Good for my business, good for the shipping business in general." He glanced at his empty glass, then into her eyes. "Besides, it's turned into an unexpected and very great pleasure."

The unexpected and very great pleasure led to another round of drinks, which Braithwaite would not let Julie pay for—"You've brightened my day, dear girl! Made me the envy of every man in the pub. I insist!"

"Do you know Mr. Goff at Hercules Maritime?"

"Robert? Speak with him almost every week."

"You deal directly with the ship's agents rather than with Mr. Wood?"

"Certainly. No reason to include Wood in the details of inquiry and planning. He signs the charter parties, of course, but the sort of routine information I need—"

"Do you see Goff often?"

"No . . . I don't believe I've ever met him in person. Everything over the telephone. Strange, isn't it?" He smiled at a corner of the room. "I've been telephoning Hercules Maritime almost daily for years and know Robert's and Wood's voices intimately. But I wouldn't be able to tell you whose face those voices belonged to. I suppose I have closer acquaintance with voices and computer terminals than I have in personal life." He added brightly, "Rather sad, when you think of it."

Julie shifted direction. "That building their offices are in looks like a run-down tenement. I expected something a little more . . . business-like."

"Oh, well. That building is a Crown property. Owned by the Queen, you see, and the Windsors are notorious landlords. Everything for profit and nothing for upkeep." He waved his cigarette in a small circle and chuckled. "A metaphor for the entire nation, perhaps. Many of the buildings in this area of London make handsome profits for the royal family and the peers. Still, that doesn't prevent the Queen from asking Parliament for more money every year or two, does it?"

And then Julie came back to the main target. "How can I get in touch with Mr. Goff outside the Hercules Maritime office?"

"Eh? Oh—I see!" A long inhale and a puff of thin blue smoke as he considered. "He does have a pager number for emergencies. I suppose you could reach him on that after working hours." Casually, he lifted an address book from his jacket's inside pocket and dangled it between thumb and forefinger. "You would like to have it, of course."

"I would be very grateful."

"And discreet, dear girl?"

She gave him her warmest smile. "Very."

He smiled back. "So I've noticed."

When they finally made their way out of the New Roses to a now vacant Leadenhall Street, Julie could feel the effects of the shandies as they said good-bye, and she wasn't as alert as she should have been. It wasn't until she was in the lift up from Russell Square Station that she glimpsed a face she half noticed earlier. It had gazed into the window of a closed shop as she and Braithwaite came out of the pub. The half-turned profile had a snub nose and contrasting bulbous chin. Average height, denim jacket that verged on dressy, the man now stood at the back of the elevator and stared over Julie's head. Blue eyes. No marks or scars. Sandy hair with a slight wave. And a bland innocence in avoiding her study.

It could be coincidence. London channeled much of its human traffic through the Tube. It wasn't impossible to see the same face on a connecting train or in another station. Still, like her father, Julie was suspicious of coincidence.

The station was a short distance from London University—one of the few sections of the city she knew thoroughly. Those were streets she and Ian had walked, she painfully in love with the older youth who introduced her to London, to the noisy and crowded student pubs, to passion, to sex, to loss. The streets, walks, buildings, and fences had changed little in ten years. Russell, Tavistock, and Woburn squares with their gardens and paths still evoked memories she thought were gone with Ian.

Now, instead of heading toward her room in the Russell Hotel, venerable and haunted with memories, she turned away down Bernard Street, strolling toward the worn grass of Brunswick Square. Turning left for a block, she went up Tavistock and paused to read another of the pale blue historical plaques—the site of another pub favored by Charles Dickens, the Edwin Drood. Then she crossed with the traffic light into Tavistock Square and ambled along one of the quieter paths between trimmed lawns. Pausing to glance behind, she saw a now-familiar snub nose and rounded chin near the square's gate, apparently enjoying the traffic of Woburn Place.

She meandered down the truncated streets and quiet corners that formed the grounds around London University's gray buildings. But memories of the lecture halls, of the heady joy of study for its own sake, of two lovers lingering in quiet corners had been replaced by thoughts about the man following her.

Twilight brought out the streetlights as she walked a little faster now. The massive dome and shadowy façade of the British Museum loomed ahead. Pale brick faces of well-cared-for row houses glowed with curtained windows, and even Great Russell Street was almost empty of foot traffic. She turned into a narrow lane that looked as if it led to Bloomsbury Square. But it was, she knew, a cul-de-sac with a certain garden-level address Julie had visited with all the excitement and eagerness of an answering heart. Past silent homes with an occasional "to let" notice—no emotion at all now, no sense of yearning— she walked swiftly back to the corner. The man stood motionless beside a mushroom-shaped letter drop whose red color was almost lost in the dim light.

"Why don't you ask me what you want instead of following me?"

"Sorry, miss?"

"You've been following me. Why?"

"Haven't any such thing! I live just down the street here. Just stepped out to post a letter."

"Which way down the street?"

"Right down there, if it's any of your business, miss."

"You've made it my business by following me. If I see you behind me once more, I will call a policeman."

"You haven't seen me behind you at all!"

Julie stepped quickly toward the young man and saw the start of angry fear in his eyes; it was the look of something cornered and on the edge of being dangerous. "The New Roses pub, Russell Square Station, and here. As bad as you are at this, you ought to go into another line of work."

"I don't know what you're talking about! Leave off, now—I mean it!" His hand slipped into his jacket pocket, and Julie, wary, watched his eyes and waited for that instant when a weapon would be pulled.

But he only backed away. "You're crazy, is what you are! Think this is America? I haven't been following anybody!"

"Next time, the police." She walked into the darkness between two streetlamps Behind her, a voice throaty with anger muttered, "Bloody bitch!"

X

The *Aurora Victorious* trembled from the power of its engines as it steamed slowly up the Gulf. Night had come, so humid and thick that Raiford could almost chew it. But the heat did not lessen. Like eruptions from hell, an oil field's burning gas vents flared hotly somewhere in the blackness.

First Mate Pressler introduced Raiford to the officers gathered in the dining saloon for the evening meal—"This is Pierce's stand-in. Name of Raiford." Scarcely breaking stride to nod, the dozen men gulped their food in near silence. Then half of them disappeared without a word. The rest, belching with the haste of eating, and picking their teeth with the satisfaction of being finished, moved into the wardroom for coffee or a drink so the fast-working steward could clean the saloon.

Third Officer Li smiled at Raiford and waved a hand

toward the bar. "Help yourself to drink—please to sign chit for what you take. Honor system." Scheduled for bridge duty in half an hour, Li sipped a heavy mug of coffee. "You find cabin okay? Know ship now?"

Raiford nodded, "Somewhat," and sank into a heavily padded armchair beside the Chinese officer.

One of the engineering officers—Graham Hansford—came over, drink in hand, and dropped into another chair. "Getting settled in, are you?"

"It's still a bit strange. But I'm comfortable, thanks." Raiford asked Li, "Can anyone use that ship-to-shore phone? I'd like to call home and tell them I arrived all right." As directed, he had e-mailed Stanley Mack just before boarding the ship's launch. But Julie should be called, too, and his cell phone had fallen mute.

"Oh, yes. You buy a calling card from purser—fifty dollars for two hundred units. Very expensive. Satellite relay."

Hansford nodded. "Two hundred units translates into about fifteen minutes. Cheaper than the six dollars a minute without one, but you'll want to use off-peak hours even with a card. For the Indian Ocean region, that's 03:30 to 07:30, Greenwich time." He added, "The ship's e-mail is fifty cents a kilobyte. Use Pierce's account number—you'll get billed when you leave ship. E-mails queue up and transfer out three times a day at off-peak hours: 07:35, 19:35, 23:35 GMT. There's fax, too—six dollars a page, whether it goes through or not."

Li giggled. "You pay for everything except quarters and

three meals a day." He added, "And coffee—owners still supply coffee."

"Though how bloody long that will last, who knows. Bloody crew even has to pay for their television. Entertainment fee, the sods call it, and blasted few of the films are in Chinese."

Laughing as if it were a joke, Li agreed. "Owners give you money and take your money. Sometimes more take than give."

"Ya—and Li, you poor sod, you're ripped off worse than we are." Hansford rubbed a finger down his long nose and winked at Raiford. "Li's new aboard—they got him for half the pay of the previous third officer. A real bargain, our Li is, aren't you, lad?"

"They tell me take the job or leave it." He laughed again. "I take it."

"Got taken is more like."

"You're Rossi's replacement?"

Hansford looked sharply at Raiford. "Knew him, did you?"

Raiford guessed that the second officer had been talking. "No. His parents phoned me in the States. They asked me to find out what I could about his accident." He shrugged. "The owners didn't tell them much about it, I guess."

Hansford grunted and studied the toe of his shoe.

"They also wanted anything personal he might have left. You know, some souvenir of their dead son." A violin in the background would have been helpful. "Any idea where his personal effects might be stored?"

Hansford's voice was abrupt. "If Rossi left anything personal, the captain would have sent it to the home office for forwarding. Any clothes he left are probably in the slop chest by now." The mate crossed bony knuckles around one knee and leaned back against the pull of his arms. "Li, here, never met Rossi. I knew him, though. Many a time he sat right there where you're sitting and I sat right here. We tossed down our share."

"Did you see his accident?"

"No. But I was at the funeral—nice one. You can tell his parents that. All hands at services, even the Muslims, and Captain Boggs reading Psalm 23." Hansford added, "Had to use the Liberian flag, though. But that's close to the Stars and Stripes, right? Guest of honor didn't seem to mind, anyway."

Raiford had to agree that the substitute flag made little difference to Rossi. He stared at the black circle of coffee in his mug. It tilted very slightly first one way and then the other. The motion was almost imperceptible. Except for the trembling of the deck, Raiford would not know they were under way. "Was the weather rough when he fell?"

Hansford tugged at a lock of his curly dark hair as he thought. "Can't recollect." He called across the wing of his chair. "Mr. Pressler—Mr. Raiford here wants to know was the weather rough when Rossi had his accident."

The lounge was suddenly and silently alert. The squat man, a highball glass dwarfed in his meaty fist, slowly looked up from the magazine he leafed through. "Rough? Neither rough nor calm. Average, I'd say. Why?"

"Says he wants something to tell Rossi's parents."

"Well, Mr. Raiford, tell them it was a day like any other." The man's lips stretched in a grin that showed stubby teeth with wide gaps. "That's how people die, right? On days like any other?" Then, "Speaking of which, you ready to go down in the tank tomorrow morning? Solenoid's out on one of the relay switches. Mr. Hansford, there, can show you the way."

"Me? Bloody hell!"

"Yes, you, Graham me lad. The job calls for an engineer to accompany, and Chief Engineer Bowman gave me your name. So direct any complaints to him. Besides, it's time someone from engineering did some damned work around here—earn your bleeding pay, like."

"Gawd, I hate going down in the tanks."

"Don't know anybody likes it. But we can't have our brand-new electronics specialist croak off, can we? You keep him out of trouble. And while you're at it, you can look over the plates for cracks. Have your work party at the hatch of number two center tank at oh eight hundred. With Drager gear."

"Oh, gawd."

Raiford drained his cup. "I'd better do some reading."

"So you should, Mr. Raiford." Pressler smiled again. "You want to be ready—don't want to spend time fumbling about down there. Mr. Li, speaking of time, it's nearing eight bells. Haul your arse up to the bridge."

"On my way, sir."

Woody, the Taiwanese deck steward, had pulled heavy drapes across the windows to prevent light from escaping forward. The day couch was now a large, freshly made bed with sheet and light blanket neatly turned down at one corner. A pitcher of cold water stood sweating next to an upturned glass behind the rail of the small table. The lamp glowed softly, promising rest, which, Raiford was aware, he needed very much.

Setting his travel clock for two forty-five, Raiford put himself quickly to sleep by reading wiring diagrams and specifications for the loading control system. When the alarm gave its muffled rattle beneath his pillow, he dragged himself to a sitting position and rubbed his thumbs into puffy eyes. Then he opened his door slowly. The corridor was illuminated by low-wattage bulbs in wire cages placed every twenty feet or so along the walls. The pungent odor of oil was gone now, though the protective strips were still laid over the green carpets. In the stillness, he felt more than heard the engine's throb far below. But except for an occasional slow creak of metal or the steady wash of the ventilation system, there was no sound. Hansford had said they were steaming at a slow twelve knots—"mooring point won't be clear of traffic before thirteen hundred hours"—and it would take three hours more to tie up and bring the hoses to the manifolds before they could start filling tanks. "Gives us the whole morning to check out the relay switches. We won't stay in the tank that long, though. Beastly place!"

Raiford's feet were silent on the carpeted stairs leading down to the lower bridge deck and its wardroom. In the dimness, the coffee urn's light glowed red, warning that someone would probably come by for a cup before the second watch reported for duty at 03:45.

Directions for use of the Inmarsat-A telephone were taped to the set. Turning it on, Raiford let the satellite telephone warm up for a few seconds as he read his new calling card with its directions for use. From this corner of the world, his voice would be transmitted through at least two satellites. Figure ten or eleven hours' difference. Using the time-chart hanging on the bulkhead, it was hard to tell exactly where the hour line ran through the Gulf. But it should be around five or six in the afternoon in Denver, and Julie could be working late. But the only response was a digital voice that apologized and told the caller to please leave a message.

He did: the Indian Ocean Region Code and the seven-digit ship ID number. Then he dialed again. This time he spoke to Julie's personal answering machine. "Hi, Julie—it's knight-errant father. Here's the calling code in case you need to reach me." He repeated the numbers, then dialed a third time. This was to Julie's mobile telephone, and, after several rings, her voice answered, "Hello?"

"Hi, Julie."

"Dad! Is it you? How are you?"

"Fine. How are things in Denver? Anything new?"

"I'm in London—got in yesterday."

"London . . . ! Hercules Maritime's offices?"

"Yes. They didn't give me much, but I do have a lead to one of their clerks who might help. I'll try to set something up with him this evening." She didn't mention the man who had followed her. Her father would have enough on his mind without worrying about that. Besides, she could take care of herself. "It seems like you've been gone for ages."

"Yeah, it does—only another thirteen days, six hours, and thirty-four minutes to go, but who's counting? Still, it's good I came—there's something here. I ask a question about Rossi and people get tighter than a lawyer giving free advice. See if you can locate Rossi's footlocker. The captain thinks it was sent to the home office to be forwarded to his parents." A movement in the passageway caught his eye. "Can't talk much now but here's the ship's calling codes if you need to reach me. Can't rely on my cell phone. For backup I'll use e-mail or fax to the office." He was repeating the ship's numbers when Shockley, not surprised to see the Inmarsat in use at this hour, came in. Raiford said a tender good-bye to Julie—not entirely for Shockley's benefit—and nodded hello as he hung up. "Calling my daughter. Let her know I arrived okay."

The pudgy man yawned and nodded. "Spend half my bleeding pay on calls to me family." He rattled in the breadbox for a stale roll to go with his coffee. "Don't forget to log your calls in the book, there. Purser gets huffy if the user log don't square with his record of calls."

Shortly after a hurried breakfast, Raiford jogged down the long deck toward Hansford and two seamen standing near the hatch. The sun, which had been gigantic and scarlet as it shouldered through the mauve band of dust and haze that was the morning horizon, was turning into a white glare that stung Raiford's eyes. Even this early, the green deck rippled with heat, and he felt as if he trotted down a long runway—broad, empty, hot—toward the cluster of men, equipment, and bicycles near the rail. Every hundred feet or so, a fire hydrant straddled the central piping, and here and there tubes, cleats, and access hatches erupted from the level surface of the deck. Beyond the pipes of the loading manifold, a low steel barrier crossed the deck in the form of a shallow V whose angle was aimed forward. Farther down toward the bow was another. Breakwaters, he had been told, to shed seawater that might plunge over the bow during storms and wash down the lengthy deck to crash into the island. But it was hard to imagine any wave big enough to rise above the ship's wide bow.

As Raiford neared the three men and the pile of gear at their feet, he saw a small, oblong access hatch laid back. Its underside, like the belly of a frog, shone dull white. A shaft of sunlight angled through the opening into a vast cavern and died out before reaching the bottom.

"How deep is that thing?"

"Thirty meters straight down." Hansford checked out Raiford's rubberized coveralls and green Wellington boots. They were the largest in ship's supply, but they were all too tight. "You look like ten kilos of potatoes in a five-kilo bag. Gloves? Got your gloves?"

"Right here. They're small, too."

"On you anything normal would be. Wearing any metal? Necklace, earring, wristwatch, whatever?"

"No."

"Good, then. Won't do to have a spark. Tank's been cleaned—all of them get washed on the ballast leg of the voyage and it's supposed to be gas-free. But they're never really safe. Look clean and peaceful and then blow up in your face over nothing." The engineering officer winked at one of the waiting crewmen, an Asian whose wide face had been badly scarred by smallpox. "Like a woman, eh, Charley?"

The man laughed and covered his mouth politely.

"This is Mr. Raiford. Charley. Sam. Both are named Wang. Cousins or some such. Most of the crew's named Wang and most are from the same village, so we just use the first names. Right, lads?"

More laughter and smiles.

"Which of you is going down with us?"

The pockmarked man bobbed his head. "I come."

"You're single and Sam's not, is that it?"

A grinning nod. "Sah!"

"All right. Let's check out the gear and get this over with."

Sam helped the three sweating men into cumbersome breathing tanks, hoses, and resuscitators. Then they loaded up with rubberized bags of equipment and vinyl-coated tools. Easing through the narrow hatch, they climbed slowly down the rungs welded to the bulkhead.

"Gawd, I hate it! Pressler knows it, too, that arse crawler. Makes damn certain the chief engineer chooses me to go down every time. I'm the one with the most experience, he says. Damn right I am. Nobody else gets a chance at any. Whoo!"

"If this is the kind of ladder Rossi fell down, I can see how it would spoil his weekend."

Hansford paused and squinted up at Raiford, mouth twisted. "Why don't you lay off Rossi? He had an accident and the poor sod's dead. For God's sake, let it go."

"I'm only asking because—"

"Because his mum and dad want to know. I understand. But what good will it do them, eh? He's dead. That's that. Dead and gone. Just leave it, can't you?"

Silently, Hansford started down again. Raiford and Charley followed, one slow step at a time.

The farther down into the fading light, the larger the vast cavern seemed. Above, a row of open Butterworth plates in the deck gave the only illumination. Raiford could see Sam's head, a black bump at the edge of the nearest circle of sky, peering down. He lowered a spare oxygen mask on a long line to dangle a third of the way down the ladder. The ports receded until they were dots of glare far above the gloom. Around the men loomed shadows of pipes and valve housings. The hull's gigantic transverse beams were as large as cathedral buttresses. Bayonets of tank washing machines rose twenty feet from the ship's bottom. They reminded Raiford of wire sculptures made of cast-off rods and piles of scrap.

Hansford had told Raiford to let him know immediately if he started to feel a bit tipsy or sleepy, or had any numbness on his skin. "Gas bubbles float about. We use the Drager gear where we can, but there's no way we can do a proper job without taking it off." Only two or three breaths of the odorless and tasteless hydrocarbon gas would knock a man out, Hansford said. Raiford should not be shy about speaking up if he felt any of the symptoms of gassing. Without a resuscitator, a man would have six minutes to get up to the deck before dying. Looking at the almost invisible top rungs of the ladder, Raiford knew no one could ever make it.

"All right, Mr. Raiford. This is the relay switch that wants looking after. Charley, you give an anchor to that fitting. I'll get the damn housing loose."

Hansford's voice was loud in the absolute silence of the steel cavern. Raiford could smell oil, but he saw none—the washing machines had scoured every angle of the dim struts and beams, steel plating, ladders and catwalks. Even any color had been washed out to leave only the hue of dead ash. And the ship's vibration, felt everywhere else, was dead here, too.

"How much oil does this tank hold?"

"Eighteen thousand tons. Want to get the clip off that lead?"

Hansford held the insulated flashlight while Raiford worked in the circle of its beam. The electrical connections to the unit were basic: circuit and grounding wires, or "earthing" as the British diagram named it. But the solenoid was crammed behind complex shielding. It had to be guaranteed against the slightest possibility of an electrical spark when the current switched on to operate its valve.

"All right, Charley. He's got it. Hand me the new unit, and

for God's sake don't drop the bloody thing or we could all be cinders."

Even deeper recesses were below them. From the lifeless gray where they worked, dark caverns led into almost total blackness. A small walkway ran across the tops of the transverse beams, and ten or twelve feet below that was the final steel plating of the double hull that held out the sea and gave support to the network of pump hoses and siphons.

The only sound was the scuffle of Wellies or the whisk of rubberized cloth. Raiford tied off the electrical leads and tightened their clamps, careful not to drip sweat from his face onto the connections. Then he held the light while Hansford replaced the shockproof housing over the unit.

"Good—let's give her a test." He unclipped the portable VHF radio from his belt and keyed the transmit button. "Mr. Bowman? Give it a try, sir."

There may have been a faint click from the replacement unit, but Raiford couldn't be certain. The only noise he was conscious of was the thud of his own heartbeat in his ears.

A tiny voice said, "Well done."

"All right! Let's get the hell out of here." Hansford quickly but carefully placed his coated tools into the rubber bag. "Charley—stow your gear and . . . Charley?"

The man, head lifting slowly at his name and mouth sagging open, gazed dully at Hansford with glassy eyes.

"Jesus! Gas!" Eyes stretched with fear, Hansford jammed his mouthpiece between his lips and stumbled for the ladder, leaving Charley to waver and sag against the beam. As the mate climbed frantically, Raiford, sucking on his own air tank, crammed Charley's rubber mouthpiece up to the man's lax jaw and slung him over his shoulders in a fireman's carry.

Thighs straining against the tightness of his coveralls, he raced after Hansford. At first the seaman's weight wasn't much. But with more steps he felt heavier and heavier until Raiford's legs burned with every lunge. The mouthpiece constricted his breathing until it strangled the gasps of air he sucked frantically through the narrow hose. And he could use only one hand on the rails. The other clamped Charley's breathing tube into the now-unconscious sailor's mouth. As Raiford slowly rose above the steel plates and beams, he stared at his hand to will its accuracy as it quickly released and slapped for the next rung. His body clenched tighter and tighter against the outward pull of the weight across his shoulders and against the thought that his hand, clumsy and sweaty in its ill-fitting glove could reach for a thin steel bar and miss. And, as if malignantly reading his thoughts, his fingers stubbed on the next rail and he felt himself flail backward and grabbed wildly with his other hand. The breathing tube slipped from Charley's mouth, but Raiford—jerked straight-armed and off-balance over the darkness below—clung motionless for a long instant. Then, curling his chest and stomach muscles against Charley's weight, he blindly pulled back close to the ladder and stuffed the mouthpiece back into Charley's face. Then he started up again toward the oblong glare that was still so small and distant.

He was finally nearing the top when he saw Hansford

descending, tugging the emergency mask at the end of its long line.

"Can you put this on him?" Hansford's voice was raw with the struggle of his own climb.

Raiford, breathless, shook his head, forcing the tearing muscles of his thighs to make the last 30 rungs . . . the last 15 . . . the final 10. . . . He spit out his mouthpiece and pumped air into his burning lungs and pushed his trembling legs up the last 5 rungs.

Hands clawed at Charley's body and hauled the weight off Raiford as he shoved himself through the hatch. The groaning effort of his final few steps was loud in his ears, but he did not know that the rasping noise was his. He collapsed facedown on the green steel plates, no longer feeling the rip of his thigh muscles, no longer staring at the slap of his stiffened and aching fingers on the steel bars. Gradually, the heat of the deck burned through the numbness of his flesh and he rolled over, squinting and blinking against the hazy glare to suck hot air deeply into his chest as the tight overalls clamped against his heaving ribs.

"Raiford—you okay?" Hansford looked up from the prone Charley. "Any gas?"

He shook his head. The heat of the deck burned into his quivering and jumping muscles. It was hot—hot enough to sting even through the heavy rubber cloth—but it loosened his strained thighs and eased the pain of flesh that had been asked to do too much.

"He's coming around. Charley's coming around."

Sam, eyes bulging with fear and shock, said something in Chinese to the sprawled man. Charley gave a faint groan.

"All right, Charley—you're going to be all right. We'll get you to hospital chop chop."

Something weak and strangled in Chinese to the hovering Sam who answered.

Two small figures were running from the distant white tower. A collapsed stretcher bounced between them. Hansford was saying something else into his radio as Sam called in Chinese to the running figures. Charley grunted deeply, curled onto his side, and vomited onto the sun-baked steel. Raiford stared at the steam that rose from the cooking puddle.

XI

Julie called Robert Goff's cell phone a little after eight, telling its message center her hotel exchange and room extension. It took ten minutes. "Is this Miss Campbell? You paged me?"

Julie explained who she was and what she wanted. Some of it, anyway. "I realize it's extremely short notice, but I wonder if I might meet you this evening."

"This evening? Now?"

"It is somewhat late and I'm very sorry. I didn't feel free to call you at work—I know how busy you are there. But I leave in a few hours and the issue really is imperative. May I buy you dinner by way of apology?"

"Well, I . . ."

"I wouldn't ask if it weren't so very, very important."

"Well . . ."

"Mr. Wood told me you would know details of the ship's operations."

"Mr. Wood said that?"

"He said you receive the ship's daily reports."

"Well, yes. But I've already dined."

"Perhaps an after-dinner drink, then? Is there a pub conveniently near your home? You see, I fly out before your office opens tomorrow, and it's very important that I speak with you. And, again, I apologize."

"You're American, aren't you?"

"Yes."

That seemed to decide it. "All right—the Two Dukes, just across from Neasden Station. That's on the Jubilee line between Wembley Park and Dollis Hill."

The silence left by the departing train accentuated the station's emptiness as well as the neglect and grime of an overused and underfunded public service. The few passengers headed toward metal stairs posted with notices to alert security about anything suspicious. Julie paused in front of the schedule of trains to let them pass. No face looked familiar; all seemed caught in their own worries. But to be certain, she walked away from the pub. Circling a block, she crossed the street and approached the Two Dukes Free House from the other direction. Its dangling street sign, lit by lights from above, showed on one side a rosy face that, despite poor drawing, looked like John Wayne wearing a kerchief and cowboy hat. The other side displayed an ebony and whitely grinning face, presumably the other duke: Duke Ellington. The owner apparently believed his customers found the royalty of entertainment more convivial than the entertainments of royalty.

The L-shaped room was plain and stark. Scarred wooden tables outnumbered the three or four booths. Harsh lighting showed dull yellow walls and a dado of worn scarlet flocking. A mix of black and white faces, mostly men, gathered in quiet laughter and talk. Against a far wall stood a row of the usual fruit machines flickering and chattering in electronic voices—a parrot: "Avast matey, win the treasure!" From a busty cartoon, a low-pitched female voice said at intervals, "I'd like you on my star craft crew. Won't you come with me?" In the last booth, sitting alone, Robert Goff ran a nervous hand down his cropped beard and nodded hello.

Julie paused at the bar to order a lager and another round of whatever Goff was drinking. Then she sat and thanked the man again for coming out so late.

"No trouble—I mean, Mr. Wood did say I was the person to speak with, didn't he?"

"He certainly did. He admires the way you handle the ship. How long have you been with Hercules?"

"Almost five years now."

"It must be interesting work."

A deprecating shrug as he used thumb and forefinger to wipe foam from the corners of his mouth. "Gets a bit routine. After a while anything does, I suppose. But it's a sight better than the dole." His eyes, dark and haunted by some inner worry, finally met Julie's. "How are jobs in the States, miss? I mean, can a chap find some decent work there?"

"Depends on what you want and what you offer. It's a big country and there are opportunities. Why?"

"Um. I've been thinking of migrating. The States, Canada, Australia." He shook his head and drank deeply again. "The shipping industry's depressed worldwide, I know that. And I'm not sure what else I'm good for. But there's not much of a future here. Not for a man wants to do best by his family." Another drink and a long stare at the well-used table. "Still, home's home, isn't it?"

They talked through another pint about various job opportunities in America, its cost of living, the ubiquitous American violence that showed on the telly and in the tabloids. About differences in school systems and housing prices. The questions seemed to be the real reason Goff agreed to meet Julie, and she was happy to barter information. When enough debt had been established, she asked Goff about the *Aurora Victorious* and the death of Rossi.

"Yes, tragic, that. Fell down a ladder, I understand. It does happen."

"Have there been many deaths aboard her?"

"Deaths? Not as many as some. And she hasn't exploded yet, thank God. But her crew's suffered the various broken bones and lost fingers and limbs."

"I understand her electronics officer is home on leave."

He nodded. "Each officer gets thirty days' leave per twelve-month. Doesn't seem worth it to me. I mean, eleven months is a long time away from your wife and children."

"Pierce has thirty days' leave?"

"No—two weeks. Gets his thirty in two fortnights. He's only a third officer, and junior officers sometimes have to do that. Scarcely time to get to know your kids again, eh?"

"Do you know Pierce's address?"

"I should remember that. I mail his paycheck monthly . . . south of London . . . Kent . . . Rochester! Yes, that's it: Primrose, number 42, Rochester, Kent. Do you need to talk with him?"

"He might have witnessed Rossi's death—if so, I'd like a statement from him." Julie shrugged. "My company wants as complete a file as possible on major incidents. But a telephone call would do."

"No one's asked for that with any of the other deaths."

"Have other ship's officers been killed?"

"Well, no. Not on my vessels, anyway."

"That must be why they're asking—he was an officer."

"I see. Well, I don't know his number. BT information can give it right enough."

Julie thanked him with another round of lager and more information about the States. "Yesterday you mentioned something about the location of the ship when Rossi was buried. Something about it being unusual?"

"I only meant that she was out of the usual southbound lane. Most tankers between the Gulf and the Cape go inshore of Madagascar. They make better time that way—currents or wind, I believe. I don't know why the *Aurora* chose an eastern route." He shook his head. "Wasn't by my direction. Mr. Wood's, maybe. And a ship's master has some leeway for local weather, provided he don't lose time overall." He added, "Mr. Wood keeps the GPS records for all the vessels in his office."

"Can you tell me who the agent was for the *Golden Dawn*?"

"The *Golden Dawn*?" Surprise lifted his eyebrows. "I was. That is, until Mr. Wood asked for it himself."

"Wood handled that ship himself?"

"Yes. He's head of the company's tanker section. But he didn't have her for long. She went down a couple of months after he took the account. All hands, too. Found a couple crewmen a bit later—what was left of them."

"He arranged the ship's insurance?"

"Oh, certainly. Whoever handles a vessel takes care of all that. Has to—get too many agents involved and things get overlooked. It's a complex business, so the whole idea is to schedulize operations—make procedures as routine as possible so they can be checked and double-checked. Used to be one account, one agent. Now agents handle two, sometimes even three, because computers do a lot now. But things can still get bollixed up—insurance or bunkerage or shipping dates. And Mr. Wood's damn quick to give the boot to anyone gets his accounts tangled."

"Does Wood often take over a ship?"

"Only time since I've been there. At first I thought it was something I'd done—had me in a sweat, I can tell you. But it wasn't, thank God. He just wanted to see to her personally, I suppose. He's the section manger—does what he likes. And when she was lost, I was damn glad he was her agent and not me." He explained, "Not that the agent can be blamed for perils of the sea or poor ship handling. But it's a funny business. Agent gets the reputation for having bad luck with his vessels and he's on his way out the door. And won't find another open very soon."

"Do you hire officers and crew?"

"The owners place the captain, with the advice and consent of the section manager, and that's always a major confab. The captain represents the owners, you understand; he's the one responsible to them for the vessel's profit or loss. Office staff deal with recruiting agencies or sometimes unions for the crews. It depends."

"On what?"

"On the flag the ship flies. Whether or not the owners are required to have citizens of that flag or can use crews of convenience. Hercules has crews of convenience on all its vessels. It's a sight better for operating expenses."

"Did you receive any of Rossi's personal effects after his death? Letters, photographs, footlocker, that sort of thing?"

"Not I, nor would I. That's up to the ship's master. Sometimes they send the personal effects to the seafarer's home address if they know it. Or to his recruiter for forwarding. Other times they don't." He shrugged. "Put what's useful in the slop chest and bury the rest at sea with the body, I suppose."

"Is it customary to have sea burials?"

"Oh, yes. Custom of the sea for centuries. No law against it, in international waters."

Julie asked a few other questions, general ones about being an agent and about the tanker business. Questions that, in Goff's memory, might blur what she had focused on. Then she gave the man tips about writing various chambers of commerce and what regional newspapers to pull up on the computer for current information. It wasn't much help for a man who wanted to emigrate, but it might come in handy if anyone at Hercules Maritime ever found out about Goff's conversation with her.

XII

Even the carpeted stairs pulled at Raiford's sore thighs as he went down to the lower bridge deck. A long soak in a hot shower had washed a lot of pain from his strained muscles, but he knew it was going to take a couple of days for his legs to recover completely.

Not that he was suffering as much as Charley. As he tapped on the open door of the hospital room, Raiford could hear the man's heavy, raw breathing. A single spartan bunk rested atop a chest of wide, gray metal drawers. The room also contained a small stainless steel cabinet with shelves filled by bottles and bandages. Its metal top held a steel washbowl and a well-used copy of the *Shipmaster's Medical Guide*. Except for the panting sailor, the white room was vacant. Charley's skin was as frail and sallow as a plucked chicken's, and the bones of his chest showed in dim shadows. At the sound of the tapping, he slowly turned his head.

"You feeling better now, Charley?"

The pockmarked face twisted painfully into something like a smile that showed crooked teeth. "Thank you, Mr. Raifah. Thank you very much."

"No problem. Couldn't leave you down there, could we? Might spoil the oil."

"Thank you very much!" Tears made his dark eyes shiny and wet as he struggled to rise on an elbow.

"Hey, Charley, what are shipmates for?" Raiford's hand clapped on the man's bony shoulder, half spanning his narrow back.

Charley clutched at Raiford's arm as if it could keep him from sinking. "Thank you, sah!"

"All right, all right. That's enough now, Charley. You're wrinkling my skin. Anybody would have done it."

"Not anybody. You. Not Mr. Hansford. You!"

"Yeah, well, Mr. Hansford went up for the oxygen mask. You still feeling a little sick? Stomach upset?" Raiford made a circling motion in front of his own stomach.

"No, no—feel good. Much better. Go to work very soon. Get up very soon!"

"Glad to hear it. Is there anything you need? Something I can get for you?"

"No—all okay now."

"Fine. I have to report to Mr. Shockley, now, but I'll come by later, okay? Make sure everything's okay with you."

"Okay, Mr. Raifah—thank you!"

Raiford drew his arm out of the man's fevered clutch and gave a long sigh as he closed the door. For a minute there, he thought old Charley was going to pry himself off the cot and offer a big fat kiss. It figured that the guy would blow the rescue all out of proportion—it was his life. Still, Raiford felt pretty good about being a hero to Charley. The look in the man's eyes brought back memories of the awe and wonder in the eyes of kids spilling onto the football field for autographs after a game. "Chin strap? Can I have your chin strap?" What did a kid do with a collection of sweaty, slobbery chin straps?

Hansford's eyes had not held awe and wonder. They had been full of terror as he realized that a bubble of gas had drifted as near as Charley and could snare him next. And the engineer had run blindly. He tried, later, to make Raiford—and maybe himself—think that he had scrambled up the ladder for the oxygen mask. But oxygen wasn't needed. They had the Drager gear, they had the resuscitators. And that's what really saved Charley, even more than the long, nightmare climb. No, if Hansford had been capable of thought at all, he had been thinking only of himself, and that told Raiford how much he would be on his own in any other emergency. Still, remembering Hansford's bulging, unseeing eyes, he wasn't going to blame the engineering officer. The only reason Raiford had stayed behind to pick up Charley was because he was too dumb to know better. Maybe if, like Hansford, he'd seen what the gas could do to a human being, he would have had the same ungovernable terror.

While Sam had not said anything about Hansford leaving Charley to die, he had knelt on the hot steel beside the clenched and retching sailor and stared at the engineering officer with openmouthed dismay. And Hansford had escaped into his quarters as soon as possible, leaving Raiford to explain to the first mate in a few exhausted phrases what had happened.

Mr. Pressler, medical officer by virtue of his rank, had not summoned his best bedside manner for Charley. "Right. Well, haul the bugger down to hospital. I'll take a look at him there—too damned hot out here. Shot of paregoric'll have him back to work soon enough. Where the hell do you think you're going, Mr. Raiford?"

"Change clothes."

"Be damned quick about it. We'll be tying up within the hour. I want you in the pump control room with Mr. Shockley when lading commences, hear me?"

"Aye, aye, Cap'n."

"I'm not the goddamned captain, you lubber! I'm the first mate!"

The second officer was not enthusiastic about having Raiford join him. "Mr. Pressler sent you here?"

"Told me to stick with you. Said you couldn't function without my skill and talent."

"Damned if he did!" The pudgy man stared in shock first at Raiford then at the dials and lights as the oil flowed into the tanks. Finally, he muttered, "The chief steward tells me you were quite the hero this morning."

"Shucks, it warn't nothing."

Another noncommittal sound. Shockley touched the dials in answer to a flicker of red and green lights. "That relay in tank five seems to be working now."

"Good. Hate to think that little trip was for nothing."

"Yes." The second officer kept his eyes on the readouts and dials, glancing now and then at the Sweding machine's load projections. But the defensive angle of his shoulders showed he was very much aware of Raiford. "Where did you say you worked before coming aboard?"

"I didn't. I'd been out of a job for six months. Got laid off, saw an ad that said electrical engineers were needed aboard tankers."

"So you decided to play jack-tar for a while."

"It's a job. Free room and board and the pay's not bad."

"That's what we're all in it for, isn't it? The money." He fine-tuned another dial and glanced at Raiford. "A river of money, this business. And we all need more. Never seem to have enough, eh?"

Raiford held his gaze. "A man can always use a bit more."

After a pause, Shockley nodded. "Yeah. We all can." Then he spoke as much to himself as to Raiford. "Damn right we all can!"

Raiford wasn't quite sure what that exchange had been about. At first he sensed an implied meaning, a vague offer of some kind for some service equally vague. But then Shockley fell silent, turning from Raiford to keep his attention on the display boards. After a long while, the Sweding machine gave a readout and the pudgy man said, "We're reaching ullage on all tanks."

Whatever made Shockley defensive and sullen began to ebb, revealing a glimmer of the man's pleasure in doing his job well. "Now we leave just enough air space for the cargo to expand when we reach the tropics." He rattled numbers on the keypad. "Has to be exact—too much space and we go light on the cargo and lose money. Doesn't take much, either. A meter low in each of those tanks adds up to a lot of tons of oil. Owners get damned upset if that happens. Too little space and the expansion could make the old *Aurora* split her seams. It's all programmed in the computer by the chaps ashore, but I like to check anyway. I mean, their arses aren't sitting on all this oil, are they?"

"How long before the computer does it all?"

"And I'm out of a job?" Shockley shook his head. "Damned close now. Endangered species, that's what we are. But nobody's looking after us because of that." The sullenness returned. "We have to look out for ourselves."

"So I better not plan on long-term employment?"

"Your kind will do all right. Always do."

"My kind? What's that mean?"

Whatever Shockley had been about to blurt, he changed his mind. Instead, he said, "Computer whizzes. Electronics specialists. Automation means a vessel can't do without you. Me, I'm just here to keep an eye on the vessel and these bloody machines. Wouldn't know what the hell to fix if one acted up."

The Sweding machine gave another chuckle and burped out a sheet of printout. Shockley ripped it off. "Here's our final projection and I have to get it up to the bridge. Why don't you go up on deck and watch the port inspector verify the ullage?"

They both found relief in leaving the pump control room and each other. The heat of afternoon had thickened the sea haze. A misty, pearly glare surrounded the *Aurora Victorious* and two far-off tankers at their floats. The shore was seven miles distant and invisible, but at some vague distance, the Ju'aymah oil platform was a dark line pimpled with scattered buildings and linked by causeways to clusters of oil meters and manifolds. Light standards were spaced along the sea island's edges, and a tall mast bearing a flashing red light warned aircraft. The surrounding horizon was lost in the gauzy light. One of the neighboring ships, deceptively small against the milky nothingness where the horizon should have been, rode empty and high. Reflected on the level sea were the red of its lower hull and, in the black paint above, the white of its load lines. Another tanker was nearing full, its black flank standing less than half as tall as the empty ship. Raiford figured his own vessel must look like that by now: the lowest part of the main deck appeared to be almost level with the water, and a lot of the white load markings on her bow had sunk out of sight beneath the ocean's flat surface.

Third Officer Li stood in the shade of the island, dressed in a yellow T-shirt, white ducks, and a sun-faded gimme cap that said MOPAR. He greeted Raiford with a smile that hinted he, too, had heard what happened. "Soon we start voyage back—much chipping rust, much painting."

"That's what we do on the way back?"

"Oh, yes. Maintenance schedule must be followed. Shore office sends it out, tells us what to take care of now, what to do tomorrow. Always, with a full ship, we clean and paint." He explained, "Full tanks are much safer than empty ones for chipping and sanding—not so much fumes."

Far down the green deck shimmering with heat, the tall figure of Captain Boggs, the squat one of Pressler, and two or three crewmen watched a kneeling shape reach an arm into an open Butterworth plate.

"What's that guy doing?"

"Oil terminal inspector. Measures empty space above the level of cargo—learns how much oil exactly in each tank."

"All the computers and electronics and flow gauges we have, and that guy still has to measure the oil with a dipstick?"

Li laughed. "Shipper's final check. Not too easy to give false reading on a stick. Also tells Captain Boggs how much oil to jettison in bad weather."

"Why's that?"

"Heavy seas. If a vessel rides too low, no freeboard. Can ship water into boilers, can break apart. Very dangerous, too much load in heavy seas." He pointed to the high-riding tanker on the horizon. "You see the freeboard lines and Plimsoll mark on that bow over there?"

Raiford spotted the short white horizontal load lines that made little ladders above and below a white circle that was bisected by its own longer horizontal line. "What do you call that? The Plimsoll mark?"

"Yes. Look at that other ship. Almost all its freeboard lines are under water. Plimsoll mark's right at water. Very loaded vessel, like us. Top is load line for tropical seas. Next line, just at water, is load line for summer seas. Below is load line for winter seas. Before, we use winter load line going around Cape Town. Now we use the summer line to carry more oil. Good for owners but not so good for a safe ship." The slight man's shoulders rose and fell with an acceptance of his fate and of decisions out of his hands. "It's a gamble. If the sea gets too rough, we jettison enough oil to stay afloat. Maybe five hundred tons, sometimes a lot more." He laughed and covered his mouth. "A lot of money. But Confucius say, better half a load than no load at all."

"Confucius said that?"

Another laugh. "Maybe."

It was a glimpse behind the man's reserve to a humor that Raiford had not suspected. It told him that the third mate had, indeed, heard of the morning's adventure and was now willing to admit this giant Westerner into a level of acquaintance generally denied other round-eyes. "Well, it's nearly October. What's that, springtime in the Southern Hemisphere?"

"Yes. Not so bad as July and August. We have a good northern monsoon down to the equator and calm seas. But below Madagascar maybe storms. Big waves—big!" His gesture motioned toward the island towering above them. "So big they break the glass on the navigation bridge!"

Raiford looked up the tall face of white steel with its tiers of square, sun-glinted windows. "That's fifty feet up."

A happy smile. "Oh yes."

"You have seen a wave that high?"

"Oh yes. First trip when I was a cadet. Scared me very much!" He pointed toward the bow and made a rolling motion with his hand. "Came over the bow, bam! Smashed glass in the bridge. Killed the helmsman. Hell of a mess."

"This was on a tanker like this?"

"Oh yes. *Aramco Sheik.*"

Raiford looked up again. Maybe fifty. Forty feet for sure. With him on this tub? Suddenly, despite its size and solidity, the tanker did not feel so large and safe.

The cluster of men began to separate. The inspector, the captain, and a crewman headed for the ladder that hung over the side down to the landing platform and a motor launch moored to it. The first mate strode quickly toward the island. Other hands began closing and dogging the inspection plates, and another mounted his bicycle for a sprint toward Li and an exchange of rapid Chinese.

"We drop lines now," said Li. "Get under way." He seemed eager to have the ship free of its moorings. It was a mood that the rest of the crew shared. Almost imperceptibly, following a brief scramble of crewmen, bleated commands from the Tannoy, and a splash of heavy mooring lines, the ship, with a deep blast of its hoarse whistle, began to swing through the flat sea. It created a heavy bulge of water that gradually turned into a deep wake fanning away from the moving hull in oily undulations. As the massive craft turned, Raiford could make out through the haze on the western horizon something congealed that drifted past in dimly marbled patterns. Sometimes it was white, sometimes pale brown. Then he recognized it: sand and rock where the desert came down to the water's edge. It was all he saw of the Kingdom of Saudi Arabia.

XIII

Julie used five minutes of the stripe on the back of her BT telephone card before she located a number for Reginald Pierce on Primrose Lane, Rochester, Kent. By then, it was almost eleven at night and too late to call. All the books on "How to Be a Detective" offered techniques for the care and handling of interviewees, and ringing a telephone so late in the evening was not highly recommended.

She transferred lines at Oxford Circus for Victoria Station, letting the first train pass to note if any other passenger stayed behind on the vacant platform. On the following train, she moved rearward through three or four of the almost empty cars and exited just as the doors were closing at the next stop. Then she caught the next train, scanning the few passengers for any familiar face. All the standard maneuvers told her she was clean.

At Victoria Station, she dropped ten pence into the turn-stile that guarded the stairs down to the women's loo. This late, it was empty of all but a few bundles of rags sleeping here and there on the ill-lit landing or against the glaring white tiles of the washroom. She took her time, listening for footsteps on the echoing floor. Climbing up the stairs, she paused inside the turnstile to survey the vast and cold station with its closed shops and slowly moving janitors. Their wide brooms slid noiselessly across empty concrete floors. Half shadowed against distant closed shop fronts, an armed policeman rocked slowly back and forth on tired feet.

Departure times and station names on the flutterboard listed the next train to Rochester at 04:59—a milk run that stopped at every station. Flickering lights on the notice board monotonously telegraphed its messages, among them the familiar "Delays Southeast Due to Leaves on the Line." Another string of glowing letters stated that morning expresses to Dover started at 06:00 and ran every thirty minutes through the rush hours, stopping at—among other stations—Rochester. Julie noted a couple of likely times and then went back down the wide and echoing stairs to the Tube to feed her day pass into the turnstile slot. The little card did not pop up on the other side of the gate this time. Julie glanced at the clock over the closed ticket windows: 23:58. This long day's pass had expired.

A hazy midmorning sun brought out bands of yellow leaves that marked the hedgerows. Between them, the fields were bright green with recent rain or plowed to bare, dull earth that waited for winter seed. Pale gray sheep dotted gentle emerald hills, and then the farmland would disappear behind an abrupt blur of stained and mossy brick. The train sped past long and narrow gardens serving row homes whose back doors faced the railway. Next would come a cluster of apartment façades with blank and curtained windows overlooking the track, followed by the sudden and close graffiti on retaining walls and concrete platforms. Smaller stations clattered past the windows, and then they lurched and rocked across rail junctures through thinning houses and into the green countryside again.

It took a full hour to reach Rochester. Once a major port, the small city perched on the high banks of the slow Medway River. The train curved and slowed as it crossed a trestle bridge over the muddy flats and brown water of the river's estuary. A handful of tired-looking coastal freighters and lines of grimy barges were anchored at the sides of the channel. On the far shore, a large and modern marina held rows of pleasure craft—sail and motor—all battened against autumn weather and looking lifeless on the flat water. The south bank rose steeply, held by stone retaining walls. Roadbeds angled up between redbrick buildings toward the tall remnant of a shattered stone keep that lifted above slate roofs like a broken, yellowed molar. Julie's guidebook said the fortress had been founded by the Romans, built by the Normans, and destroyed by Cromwell.

Rochester platform, like most of the others, was short on paint but long on litter and warning posters. At midmorning, with outbound trains almost empty, Julie was one of only four adults to alight in the thin sunshine and damp, chilly air. The small group made its way through the station to the cul-de-sac that opened on a busy thoroughfare. Two of her fellow passengers were women, one white-haired and bent with osteoporosis, the other heavyset and wrestling two small children. The only male was a teenager with a half-shaved scalp and gold rings dangling from his ears, nose, and eyebrows. All of which made Julie feel better about being followed. If the punk rocker was a tail, he wouldn't be hard to see; if either of the women were, she could outrun them.

A small knot of drivers stood out of the wind near a line of cabs, smoking and talking. As Julie neared the first car, a beefy figure raised his eyebrows. "Need a taxi, miss?"

The red-faced driver knew where Primrose Lane was—"A bit west, miss. Not too far, you'll see"—and talked almost as fast as the meter ran about the local landscape and what Julie might be doing in Rochester. Only half listening, Julie said yes, she was American; yes, it was her first visit to the town; yes, the castle was an interesting ruin. No, she did not know that Charles Dickens had spent a good part of his childhood here.

"You'll have to see the Dickens Museum, you will, miss— just down the High Street from the station. People come from all over to see that. And the Dickens festivals. Two of 'em: Christmas Festival in December, Summer Festival in June. Quite the affairs, both, but my favorite's the Christmas Festival. People all dressed in the costume of the day, music, food—"

The scratchy voice described that festival then shifted to the Summer Festival and listed its virtues as the cab swerved through automobile and bus traffic, lorries and vans, bicycles and crossing pedestrians heading to work. Up a steep hill, past wide football fields into neighborhoods of row houses, then half-timbered duplexes with small gardens, larger single homes with deeper lawns and taller fencing, and an occasional estate sheltered behind high brick walls. Finally the taxi turned into a winding lane with little traffic and few cars parked along the curbless verge. Pairs of semi-detached homes were spaced down the gently curving street. "Here you are, miss. Number 42." The cabbie was impressed by the address. "Quite the nice neighborhood your friends live in." He took Julie's money and handed her a smudged business card. "Just telephone this number for a lift back, will you, miss?"

Julie, eyes on the plain white car parked a bit down from the house, nodded. Ahead of it was another white car with a blue light mounted on the roof. On the door was a silver-and-blue seven-pointed star topped by a crown. The center of the star held a rearing white horse. Around its borders blue letters spelled "Kent County Constabulary." An impassive policeman in a dark blue uniform answered her knock. When he heard what Julie wanted, he frowned and said, "You'll wait right here, please," and closed the door.

Two or three minutes later, a short, blond man in a light brown suit opened the door to study Julie for a long moment before speaking. There was no surprise or admiration in his stare, merely assessment. "Might I ask what business you have with Mr. Pierce, please?" It was the familiar way police had of asking a question but making a demand. The corners of the man's mouth were pinched, and an unfocused, half-stifled anger radiated from him.

"I want to interview him about an accident that took place aboard his ship a few months ago." Julie showed her private investigator's identification card.

The policeman read it carefully. It bore Julie's photograph and looked very official. But it carried no legal weight at all in the States, and apparently even less in England. "Might I see your passport, please?"

Julie handed him the dark blue booklet. The man read first the identification page and then leafed carefully through the sheets for the stamps marking British Customs.

"You came in through Heathrow two days ago?"

"Yes."

"Might I ask where you've spent these last two days?"

"London. I talked to the people at Hercules Maritime who own Mr. Pierce's vessel, and to the cargo broker who handles that ship."

"And where in London are you staying, Miss Campbell?"

"Hotel Russell, Russell Square. Has something happened to Mr. Pierce?"

The policeman ignored the question. He slipped Julie's passport into his coat pocket. "I'd like a word with you, if you don't mind. Would you accompany me to the police station, please?"

She would accompany whoever had her passport. Which they both knew.

The policeman's title was inspector, his name was Moore, and his assignment was homicide. Julie could picture the blond man as a schoolchild, pink cheeked, smaller than his mates, with wide blue eyes and a round pink mouth singing in the church choir on a village Sunday. But that child had been lost somewhere and what remained was the slightly curly blond hair, thinning now, the sallow cheeks of an office dweller, and eyes whose innocence had been replaced by a flat and almost emotionless distance as he stared across a Styrofoam cup and nodded. "Go on."

"There's not much to add. Mr. Wood told me that Pierce was home on leave and Mr. Braithwaite gave me his address. I wanted to ask him what he knew about Rossi's death. You tell me he's been killed." Julie stuck to pertinent facts that left out a lot of things.

Moore started to say something when his telephone rang and he answered it with his name. Face expressionless, he asked, "What time?" And then, "A signed chit? Very well." He hung up and noted something on the same pad where he had copied information from Julie's passport and jotted as she spoke. Then the flat eyes met hers. "You breakfasted at your hotel this morning, is that right?"

"Yes."

The inspector nodded. "Your statement of your whereabouts seems to hold up, Miss Campbell." He pushed her passport across the desk. "You may go."

"I take it Mr. Pierce was killed last night. Would you mind telling me how it happened?"

He stood, brown suit wrinkled with long wear and, in the glare of the office's fluorescent lights, showing a few stains on the lapels. He opened the door with its panel of frosted glass. "The sergeant will direct you out."

"Was it an accident? Murder? Suicide?"

"Just accompany the sergeant, miss."

The sergeant, summoned by a button, took the cue. "Right this way, miss."

"I'm working on a case that might involve Pierce, Inspector. I've told you what I know. It might help me if I knew how and when he died."

The man's anger surged again and he stared at Julie for a long moment. She wasn't certain what the inspector was looking at, but the anger wasn't personal, it was general. It was the broad disgust for humanity that often came when a cop had seen too much too recently. "He and his wife and his five-year-old daughter were shot to death. You will discover that much in the tabloids shortly, I expect. Any information beyond that is the Crown's official business, for which you have no authorization. Sergeant!"

"This way if you please, miss."

The sergeant escorted Julie along the clean-swept hallway to a bomb-proofed door with a small, reinforced peephole at eye level. "One block to your right, miss, and then another right will carry you to the train station. Good day, miss."

The thick door closed behind her, a heavy lock clicking

firmly into place. So much for professional courtesy between the Kent County Constabulary and the private sector. In American movies, the police inspector was always willing to tell the PI details of a homicide, knowing that by the end of the film the PI would solve the crime for him. Unless the inspector turned out to be the bad guy, which gave a thrilling twist to what was labeled a realistic plot. Too bad it wasn't that way in life. And too bad that without local contacts, Julie wasn't going to find out any more than would be in the newspapers.

But a couple of conclusions could be drawn: First, the deaths took place last night or more likely this morning. Her alibi, as far as Inspector Moore was concerned, was the two hours between her documented presence at a London hotel and her appearance at Pierce's door. Second, a murder-suicide would not generate a need for suspects, so a fourth party must have killed the three members of the family.

The police would find out soon enough if Pierce's wife had a lover or if Pierce had an enemy or if some family dispute had boiled over into carnage. But the killer could also be a stranger who had a police record, and thus family members who might describe him had to be silenced. And the murders could be related to the death of Herberling. Maybe even to Rossi. But why? Why would Rossi's death be so important that any witnesses to it would have to be silenced? As well as any insurance detective looking into it?

Had someone been afraid that Julie would interview Pierce? That the ship's officer might let something slip about Rossi's death?

Officially, Rossi died in a shipboard accident. Such deaths happened almost every day of the year, and the evidence had been disposed of by sea burial. No one could question the cause of Rossi's death now. Even if Rossi had been murdered, there was no evidence to compel Pierce to admit to anything. Then why were he and his family killed?

The train slowed as it neared Victoria Station. The trip back had passed quickly while Julie was deep in thought. The huge dead stacks of Battersea Power Station, a glimpse of the Chelsea Bridge and the almost empty Thames below, then the slowly lurching roadbed led through a narrowing web of tracks to the square concrete piers of the platform and the train's final metallic squeal of dry brakes.

If Pierce's murder was related to Rossi, then Julie and her father were facing something much bigger than a cover-up of one sailor's death. Something that made four lives—even that of a five-year-old child—expendable. If Julie was guessing right, money was why she was followed. Money could explain one killing in New York and three in England. No weapon had been found at the scene of Bert Herberling's murder in New York, Percy had said. And she would bet none had been found here, either. But the same weapon would not be used for both killings. Each gun would have been permanently disposed of immediately after use. Wiped clean, dropped in a river, dumped into fresh concrete, buried. A professional killer would do that. A professional who charged professional fees. But if someone spent enough money to hire a killer—or was desperate enough to do it himself—that someone must have thought of the lives as an investment for a lot of profit. Because money had to be somewhere at the bottom of it. Look for the money: the First Commandment of detective work. There lay the highest probability of motive.

Julie joined the hurrying mob of passengers leaving the train. She flashed her railroad pass at the exit inspectors and then headed past a police picket toward the now-crowded stairs leading to the Victoria Station Underground. If money was at the center, then it wasn't Rossi but something he knew that had become a liability for someone. But what could the dead sailor tell anyone? As the escalator lowered her farther into the city's bowels, Julie understood that a search into Rossi's death was a profound threat to someone, and that now she and her father embodied that threat.

XIV

The vibration of its engines muted to almost nothing by the weight of its cargo, the *Aurora Victorious* followed the outbound sea-lanes toward the Indian Ocean. They passed through the busy Strait of Hormuz at night, blinking lights indicating the through-shipping lanes and the median between them, and the running lights of other ships gliding up-channel. Beyond those, just at the edge of vision, a series of flashing lights marked Quoin Island. Distant winks located headlands invisible in the black, and a faint city glow indicated the town of Bahka.

When his alarm went off in the morning, Raiford crossed another day off his calendar, leaving a week and a half to go. A faintly light-headed feeling came and went in slow rhythm, and he realized that the carpet beneath his bare feet was gently lifting and falling. The vessel had shoved into the wider reaches of the Sea of Oman and was now answering to the fading surges of the Indian Ocean beyond.

Even the air from the softly whistling vents felt different: fresher, lighter. It teased him from outside the shelter of the bridge, and apparently the rest of the crew shared the feeling. Breakfast was served even more briskly than usual, and the ongoing watch, eager to move into the routine of travel on the open sea, ate rapidly.

For Raiford, the day's schedule called for preventive maintenance on the radar equipment, inspecting the electrical connections from the scanner atop the mast to the plan position indicator on the navigation bridge. The idea, he was told by the third officer, was to do outside maintenance in calm seas and inboard work when they moved into the stormier seas below the equator. Raiford's assistant was Sam who, a few days ago, had crouched over the spasmodic Charley, wailing something in Chinese. Now he showed a gold-toothed smile that said the crew was glad to be away from the sultry confines of the Gulf too.

"Ready for work, Sam? How's Charley doing?"

"Charley fine. Back at work now."

"Already? Pretty tough man, old Charley. Doesn't he rate sick leave?"

"No sick leave. Man want pay, man work. Man get sick, man sent home. Somebody else come to take job."

"What happens if a sailor gets hurt? Loses a hand or breaks an arm?"

A shrug. "Sent ashore. Sometime no repat."

"No what?"

"Repat." Sam twisted his mouth around the awkward sounds. "Re-pat-la-tion."

"Repatriation?"

"Yes—repat! Many time hurt man is sent ashore to go hospital. But no repat."

"They just leave him there?"

A bob of the head. "No work, no pay, no repat. Must stay healthy, yes?"

"What happens if he gets killed?"

Another shrug and Sam's thumb wagging toward the ship's rail.

"Over the side?"

"Oh yes." He grinned. "No repat then, too." He led Raiford up the ladder rungs welded to the mast that capped the ship's towering island. Twenty feet above the open bridge and level with the rim of the deeply humming smokestack, they paused on a platform that had just enough space for them and the vessel's middle running light. A second, thinner mast rose another ten feet to a platform even smaller. Above that, at the vessel's topmost point, rotated the fiberglass dish of the radar scanner.

Raiford gazed aft across the stack. Beneath the thin brown smoke boiling out of the funnel, the wake foamed white and clean. Although the handrails, gritty with salt, were hot from the sun, the wind was cool and the ship's roll, scarcely felt on the decks below, was stronger up here. Even the sea looked different, no longer the thin color of the Gulf but the rich blue of deep water. A few clouds made a smudge low in the west, and three lean, gray shapes rose up and dropped rapidly over the northern horizon: ships of the US Navy headed to stations near Iraq. Against the *Aurora's* bow, long streaks of sunglinted rollers exploded in surges of spume and created arcs of white froth like tattered lace along the ship's flanks. The peacefulness of the scene contrasted sharply with the reason Raiford was aboard.

"Is that what happened to Mr. Rossi? Over the side?"

Sam's black eyes blinked and the smile was gone. "Yes."

"How did he die, Sam?"

Studying Raiford's face, the man hesitated then, clapping his palms together, he shrugged. "Fall off. Down inside. Gone."

"He fell inside the ship's storage tank?"

"No, no. Fall outside ship. Into water—inside two ships." His palms slapped together again. "Other ship, this ship. Mr. Rossi inside."

"There was another ship alongside and Rossi fell between them?"

"Yes—between! Gone, like that." His thumb wagged toward the blue-green swell of foaming wake.

Raiford climbed up the smaller mast to the radar dish. He hooked up the bypasses, uncovered, sanded, and retaped electrical connections; tightened clamps, screws, and guides against the ship's constant vibration; inspected the wires' woven sheaths and repainted them with all-weather coating. Finally he unhooked the bypasses and lowered himself through the open hatch of the crow's nest and down to the lower platform where Sam waited with tools and equipment.

"Why was that other ship so close to this one, Sam?"

"We off-load. Small tanker."

"You were transferring crude? At sea?"

"Yes. Happens alla time. Small tanker carry oil into place we too big to go."

"I see." Then, "Did you have a funeral for Mr. Rossi?"

"Funeral?"

"Ceremony—everybody get together on deck and say a few words about him."

"No. What for? Mr. Rossi, he gone."

It took until early afternoon to finish the radar circuit. Raiford traced the wires down their conduits, through the intricacies of the wave guide to the transmit/receive unit. There, capacitors had to be checked, connections cleaned and tightened, any vibration-frayed insulation taped or replaced and sealed. Then it was the turn of the radar unit's voltage regulator and generator, and finally into the navigation bridge and the plan position indicator where the bright streak of the radar beam swung in fading circles around a screen.

Raiford did not ask Sam more questions. And the sailor volunteered nothing more. In fact, the closer their work carried them to the navigation bridge and the officer and crewman on watch there, the smaller and quieter the sailor became. Ultimately, he was a voiceless satellite in Raiford's broad shadow, handing a screwdriver or a pair of strippers, stepping back quickly when he thought he might be in the way.

Mr. Pressler, rubber-soled shoes squeaking on the deck's paint, strode from one wing of the bridge to the other, glancing at the Decca navigator, the automatic helmsman, the wind indicator, and aft at the trail of smoke from the stack. Then starting back across the bridge again.

"Sam, hand me that coupler there, will you? That blue one."

Anxious in the presence of the first officer, the sailor darted across the bridge for the coupler just as Pressler, eyes on the horizon, turned to pace back. Unseeing, he bumped into the seaman and tripped against the control panel, his elbow banging loudly.

"Goddamn!" Pressler's thick fist clubbed down on Sam's shoulders and knocked the smaller man flat. "You goddamned slope-headed mule! Get the hell out of my way!" The mate kicked savagely at the stunned man, his shoe thudding solidly into flesh. Raiford heard the wind burst out of Sam's lungs. "Bloody clumsy barstid!"

"Hold it—that's enough!" Raiford pushed past the frozen duty watch to grab Pressler's heavy arm. "It was an accident, Pressler."

Turning purple with rage, the first mate wheeled to yank his arm from Raiford's fingers. "Take your hand off me, goddamn you to hell!"

"Just lay off, Admiral. It wasn't Sam's fault. It was an accident."

"You—" Pressler's mouth made stuttering noises. "I'll—" Raiford ignored the first mate and hoisted the small sailor up by an arm. "Take off, Sam. Job's done."

Eyes bulging with terror and body doubled with pain, Sam mumbled something squeaky and incomprehensible and lurched frantically through the doors to the stairway down.

"I'll—" Pressler's meaty fist completed the strangled sentence with a hard swing. His knuckles banged solidly against Raiford's head and stumbled the taller man into the bulkhead. Stumping forward on thick legs, Pressler swung again. "I'll—"

Raiford rolled off the echoing steel, elbow deflecting the grunted blow. He ducked under the mate's arm and used both legs to drive his fist up and deep into the shorter man's stomach. The stocky figure folded with a spew of breath. Raiford thudded the heel of his hand against Pressler's forehead, snapping his skull back with a grinding, cracking sound. Pressler grunted and dropped to his knees, head shaking, and broad hands spread wide against the deck. Then he lurched upward, eyes bulging and shot red with rage.

Raiford met the wild charge with a jab between the mate's flailing arms. His knuckles, calloused from karate, split the flesh at the side of Pressler's mouth with a spurt of bright blood. The mate reeled halfway back across the bridge but did not go down; he tucked his head between thick shoulders and, spitting blood, growled something primal and wordless and charged madly again.

Raiford sidestepped to whistle the edge of his hand down and through the juncture of Pressler's neck and shoulder. It chopped deeply, flipping the man's head sideways in a blur. The mate's eyes rolled back to show bright pink and his legs bent as if their cords had been cut. He hit the deck with the clang of falling bones and bounced heavily and lay still.

The bug-eyed duty watch stared openmouthed at the fallen man and then at Raiford.

"Looks like the first mate tripped, right?"

The man's black eyes blinked, but his mouth remained soundless and open.

"Call the captain to the bridge. You hear me?"

Another blink and the open mouth closed. The sailor nodded.

"Tell the captain that the mate tripped but you didn't see it happen. Hear what I'm telling you? You did not see anything."

"Yessah." The sailor, wearing dark blue coveralls and no undershirt, stared at Pressler. "He dead?"

"Sleeping. Go on, call the captain." Raiford gathered up the tool kit and pushed through the doors to the stairway as the seaman said into the intercom, "Sah? Captain sah? Bridge calling."

"Four stitches in his face and swollen like a blinking rugby ball! I could scarcely make out what he was saying. He'll be eating soup through a straw for a few days, I tell you that!" The second officer of engineering, Henderson, picked at one of the pimples hidden in his curly, dark beard as he grinned and talked excitedly.

By the evening meal, word of the first mate's injury had spread through the ship. The empty chair where Pressler usually sat at mess drew glances from the diners. Henderson said he had been called to Pressler's cabin during the second watch to report on the reading of an erratic temperature level in the propulsion gear. The mate's first words were "What are you staring at, you bloody sod!" and the man's demeanor declined from there.

"Tommy had the duty watch and swears Pressler had a fall or some such. Didn't see it, he claims. Pretty weak story and a damned strange fall, I think. But that's what Tommy's sticking to, and Pressler didn't volunteer a word about it. Just told me to be damned quick on my report and to get the hell out of his quarters."

"Too damn bad he didn't break his neck as well." The first officer of engineering ripped a slice of bread in two and spread it thickly with butter. Then he wagged the floppy slice at the younger officer. "You be certain you make your reports to me as well as him, Mr. Henderson, you hear me? He may be first officer of the deck, but by God I am first officer of engineering. If something's amiss with my turbines, I want to know about it immediately and not through the morning report. Do I make myself clear?"

"Yes, sir." Henderson shrank behind his soup spoon, his excitement gone.

Shockley, at the table's other end, leaned forward. "You were working around the navigation bridge this afternoon, Mr. Raiford. Did you see anything?"

He looked innocent and shook his head. "Must have happened after I left."

The second officer nodded. "I see."

"Pass the meat, Mr. Shockley." With Pressler absent, the first officer of engineering was senior at table. He wanted it understood that the saloon was for eating and not for gossip. If people had time for that, they could damn well do it in the wardroom.

That was where coffee was served after meals. When he chose to, the captain came from his private meal in his cabin and, with rusty cordiality, mingled with the ship's officers. Raiford had almost drained his heavy porcelain mug when Boggs, hair slightly ruffled at the back of his head as if he had been lying on it, stood for a long moment in the doorway and surveyed the wardroom. He caught the chief steward's eye and lifted a finger, then settled into an armchair beside Raiford.

Before the captain could cross his legs, the chief steward, brisk, impassive, and keeping his eyes on the tray, delivered a napkin, a spoon, one lump of raw brown sugar, and two plastic thimbles of milk. Carefully, he poured the steaming black liquid from the long-handled silver pot, deftly snipping off the thin stream with not a drop spilled on the paper doily covering the saucer.

"Thank you, Johnny."

"Sah!"

Captain Boggs completed his part of the ritual by adding one of the small containers of cream, then the lump of brown sugar, then the other container and, holding the upright spoon halfway down the shaft, stirred deliberately with his whole arm for a precise number of rotations. He tested the coffee with a sip from the spoon and set the cup and saucer on the little table in front of him.

"Well, Mr. Raiford. I hear you've had an active couple of days."

He wasn't sure which activity Boggs meant. "I sees me duty and I does it, Cap'n."

"Um, yes." The lanky man fell silent. Across the wardroom at the bar, the junior engineering officers murmured among themselves, voices blurring beneath the hiss of the ventilation system. Usually, the room was busy for about twenty minutes after supper, and then off-duty officers wandered back to their quarters, leaving the vacant room as oppressive and impersonal as a hotel lobby late at night for any who might remain. Occasionally, the younger men would gather to talk and laugh for a while in the warmer space of one or the other's cabins. Most often, the men were solitary, as if they saw one another enough during working hours and had heard each other's stories too often. But tonight the first mate's accident invaded routine, and the younger officers found they had things to talk about after all.

"The company has an agent aboard. One of our officers."

The sudden words startled Raiford. "What's that?"

"An agent. Shipping companies often detail one of the second or third officers to keep an eye on their vessels. To report on how well or ill the captain does his job. To give accounts for any delays in operation."

"I see," said Raiford. But he didn't.

"I'm not supposed to know who it is, of course."

"Ah. Well, it's not me, Captain. The only thing I know about ship operations is whether we're still afloat. We are, so I figure you're doing a good job."

Boggs nodded, the deep wrinkles at the corners of his puffy gray eyes pinching tighter. But it wasn't from smiling. Rather, he stared hard at something in the dark green carpet. "I know who our company spy is." His voice held a shrug. "He has his job, I have mine."

"I guess that's the way to look at it."

Another nod. "He does it for the bit extra in his pay envelope, of course. That, and a leg up on command when it comes time to strike for master."

Raiford nodded again.

"The owners reward loyalty. Want people to think they do, anyway. Big investment, a ship. A captain goes a long way toward making that investment pay off or not." For the first time, Boggs looked directly at Raiford, his gray eyes calculating something. "Suppose you had to choose, Mr. Raiford, between loyalty toward your rank and its responsibilities or being made redundant. Or between loyalty to your owners and the chance for a handsome bit of cash for yourself. Which way would you go?"

"Any man can be tempted. Depends on how much cash, I suppose."

"And on what the owners might want one to do for it." The coffee had stopped steaming and Boggs carefully sipped a bit of it. The cup chattered slightly as he set it back on the saucer. "Married, are you? With children?"

"Widowed. One daughter."

"Hm. Eleven months at sea year after year is hard on family life. Calls for a lot of sacrifices. From the man as well as the woman—both give up a lot."

"I can understand that."

Something in the remark stung the man. "You can, can you? You can understand that, can you?"

"Yes."

The captain's eyes shifted from Raiford and back to the carpet. The young officers at the bar began to fall silent, first one and then another yawning widely. Hansford drained his pint and nodded good night. As he left, he glanced toward Raiford and the captain. The others soon followed, leaving the wardroom empty except for the two seated men.

"Mr. Rossi's death was an accident. You know that, don't you?"

"That's what people tell me."

"Well, it was an accident. Shouldn't have happened but did."

"I've heard he either fell down a ladder or fell between this ship and another one."

Boggs stared at him for a second time, seeking something as he looked in the big man's eyes. "A ladder. He fell down a ladder."

"That's what Hercules Maritime told his parents. I guess that's how it happened."

"Yes. It is." Boggs took another tiny sip. "Mr. Pressler told me about the fight on the bridge this afternoon. Being a supernumerary and unfamiliar with the laws of the sea, you may not realize that in striking a superior officer you have committed an act of mutiny." He set the cup down with a click and cleared his throat. "As captain of this vessel in international waters, it is my duty to put mutineers in custody for trial in a suitable court." He paused, not for Raiford to reply but to let the words sink in.

But Raiford wasn't playing that game. "What about the sailor Pressler kicked? He almost killed him. What kind of act is that, Captain?"

"Any sailor on this vessel who wishes to complain about the actions of an officer can make that complaint to me. That is standard shipboard procedure and the procedure you should have followed." A hint of anger tightened the baggy flesh under Boggs's eyes and straightened him in the chair. "As captain, I decide whether and what kind of reprimand may be called for." Then the eyes wavered again. "However, Mr. Pressler has decided not to lodge a complaint against you. You will be leaving ship when Mr. Pierce returns, anyway." A deep breath and the eyes looked back at Raiford. "There will be no charges against you provided you say nothing about the incident to anyone. Is that clear?"

Raiford was damned glad he would be leaving the ship and only wished it would be in hours instead of days. "As far as I'm concerned, it didn't happen."

"Fine. I've told you there's a company agent aboard. If

he hears you talk about the incident and reports it, I will be forced to act as a captain should, regardless of Mr. Pressler's wishes. I will bring you up before captain's mast."

Raiford didn't know what that meant, but it sounded like Captain Bligh keelhauling somebody. "As long as Pressler doesn't go around half killing the crew."

"I'm sure the first mate will be more conscious of his behavior. And of your presence." The tall, thin man stood abruptly. "Good night, Mr. Raiford."

"Good night, Captain."

XV

Julie was finishing her late lunch when she felt the buzz of the cell phone clipped to her waist. Its small screen indicated a ten-digit number, probably a London telephone, but she did not know all the area codes. Paying her bill, she found a corner in the hotel lobby to return the call. A male voice on the other end quickly answered, "Yes?"

"I received a page from this number. Are you trying to reach me?"

A brief pause. "Is this Miss Campbell? The Marine Carriers Worldwide representative?"

She did not recognize the voice. It was slightly clipped and the vowels shaded toward a rounded sound.

"I'm Miss Campbell." That much was true. Mostly. "Who is this, please?"

"My name is Wilson. Mr. Wood of Hercules Maritime gave me your name. I wonder if I might trouble you for a few moments of your time."

"Certainly."

"I hope you don't mind."

"I don't mind, Mr. Wilson."

"That's very good of you, Miss Campbell. I'm calling from aboard the *Aurora Victorious*. It's about Mr. Raiford. I believe you received a telephone call from him a few days ago?"

"Has something happened?"

"There has been an accident, I'm afraid. With serious injuries."

"Oh, God! What . . . ?"

"I'm not certain of the full extent of his injuries, but we should know soon. We're in contact with the company medical officer ashore. But I hope you won't mind providing some information to facilitate his medical treatment. You see, he listed no next of kin on his employment form, so Mr. Wood instructed me to call you."

"What do you need?"

"Was Mr. Raiford employed prior to joining the *Aurora Victorious*? A previous employer might have his medical records, you see. In an emergency such as this, the medical people need the most complete information as soon as possible. Blood type, allergies to medications, history of previous injuries, that sort of thing." The voice added, "It's vital for the doctor to know, Miss Campbell."

"His medical enrollment card should be in his wallet with

his health provider's telephone number. They'll have his medical history."

"It's not there, ma'am. We've looked. To access his medical records, we need his previous employer's name. And as quickly as possible!"

"The Touchstone A—" A tiny electric shock silenced Julie as she realized she might have spoken too soon.

"That's in the States? In Denver?"

"What happened to him, Mr. Wilson? May I speak with him?"

"Thank you, Miss Campbell." The line went dead.

Quickly, she dialed the operator and, after giving her own number for billing purposes, learned that the number she had called was to a pay telephone near Piccadilly Circus. She dialed the marine operator and repeated the call numbers her father had given her for the *Aurora Victorious*, specifying person-to-person only. Waiting for the call back, she sometimes walked, sometimes stood and gazed through the lobby windows at the flow of automobile traffic outside. When her telephone finally rang, she flipped it open. "Dad?"

"This is marine operator sixty-two, ma'am. There is no Mr. Raiford at that number."

"There has to be—it's a ship!"

"They inform me there's no one by that name at that number, ma'am. I'm sorry. Would you like to try another number?"

". . . No."

Damn. Damn her father for going so cavalierly into danger. Damn herself for not thinking before stupidly answering that man's question. And damn everybody and everything because she felt the stifling, icy grip of fear and the knowledge that although she had to do something quickly to help her father, she had no idea what the something was.

Stanley Mack's voice lost it grogginess as he tried to fit pieces together. "The man who called you wasn't aboard the *Aurora*?"

"A pay phone near Piccadilly Circus."

"But he knew your father telephoned you from the ship—that's most likely where he got your number. So he must have some contact with the vessel."

Julie had already figured that out. "Mack, I need to know how I can reach him. I've tried all the numbers he gave me: the marine telephone, fax, e-mail, his cell phone—everything except carrier pigeon. I'm afraid I messed things up badly!"

"Slow down—tell me everything the way it happened."

She went through the details: the murder of Pierce and his family, the telephone voice of the man who called himself Wilson, what he'd asked and what she'd answered. "I think he was trying to determine if my dad is an operative, Mack. He recognized Touchstone Agency's name. He knew it was in Denver."

"Yeah." Then, "And they say he's not aboard ship?"

"The marine operator did. No one on the ship answers anything."

"And he used Wood's name?"

"Yes."

"That means he has a contact at Hercules. . . . All right.

159

Let me see what I can do through Marine Carriers Worldwide. They can ask to speak with the electronics officer. I'll get back to you as soon as I can."

Julie hung up. Wilson. The man called Wilson—and he knew Julie had interviewed Wood. Now he knew that her father was with the Touchstone Agency. And knowing whom he worked for, "Wilson" could guess why he was aboard the *Aurora Victorious*. Julie felt that slight physical swirl when facts suddenly tilted toward alignment. They had gotten rid of Herberling, possibly to erase any link between the *Golden Dawn* and the *Aurora Victorious*. And Pierce? The call from this Wilson had come around noon. If Wilson had driven the fifty or so miles to Rochester by, say, five or six or even seven this morning, he could easily have made it back as far as Piccadilly Circus by noon. Silence Pierce before Julie reached him. Do it quickly. No time to wait for Pierce's wife and child to be off to school or work because Julie could be on her way to talk to the man after interviewing Wood. Kill Herberling, kill Pierce, kill the wife and child unlucky enough to witness that murder. And now the killer knew that her father was an investigator. Julie felt so stupid!

The hope was that her father would be on his guard. That he would be fully aware of the suspicion and dangers he faced. He could take care of himself. Of course he could take care of himself—it wasn't his first undercover work, and the man who called wasn't aboard ship with him. Even though her father had often challenged common sense, as if his size and strength alone would be enough to lift him out of any hole, he wasn't careless. Supremely self-confident, maybe, but not careless. Those and similar thoughts offered hope against the cold knowledge that her father, so far away, was isolated with no way out.

She told herself that his mind would be working just as hers was. And if the ship-to-shore telephone was closed to him . . . If he wasn't injured and could move around the vessel . . . The office e-mail in Denver! If he had access to the ship's computer, he would use e-mail! Or the fax. But when she was back in her room at her laptop and she finally reached Touchstone's e-mail address, the only messages were routine. Irritably, she answered what demanded reply and trashed the rest. Then she spread out her notes on Herberling's file and started to comb through the information once more, focusing her thoughts on doing something constructive in an effort to deny the tug of worry.

Julie had packed abstracts of the file's contents but left the original documents in the office safe. Now she realized she should have photocopied everything and, despite its bulk, crammed it into her flight bag. But she had not. The complete documents sat safe and secure in Denver. And unavailable.

Reading through what she had, she added what she could recall from the file. She also considered the information from the different angle that Wilson's call suggested. And that was enough to give her a thread to pull.

She tried Stanley Mack again. He had not yet had a reply from Marine Carriers.

"Mack, have you come up with anything new on Captain Boggs."

"A little. You think you can reach Boggs to ask about Raiford?"

"Not likely. My guess is the ship's not answering any caller they don't recognize. Do the police have anything new on Herberling's murder?"

"Nothing." Then he added, "The *Aurora Victorious* and the *Golden Dawn*—they figure in Bert's killing as well as in the Pierce murders, don't they?"

"That's what I think, too. Listen: Herberling had a list of five names and addresses in his *Golden Dawn* files, and he drew circles around three of them: Pierce, Boggs, and one other name—the chief engineer, I think. Can you verify that from your copy?"

"Let me pull the file." Then, "Yeah—three. The chief engineer's Bowman. The two not circled are Pressler and Shockley. What, you got a photographic memory?"

For a few things, and not always the most important. "Any idea why he would mark those names?"

Mack thought a moment. "On a list like this, he usually circled things he wanted to look into. When he'd done it, he'd draw a big *X* through the circle. That way he could tell at a glance how far he'd got."

"I don't remember any *X*s."

"Nope. Means he didn't get to whatever," said Mack.

"You sent me photocopies of everything in his file, right? Nothing left out?"

"You got it all. Why?"

"Braithwaite—Hercules Maritime's London agent—told me he faxed Herberling a message concerning the *Aurora Victorious*. But it wasn't among the stuff you sent me."

"Braithwaite? The *Aurora*? Just a minute." Another hiss of empty air. "No, nothing like that in these papers. What did his message say?"

"That he was unable to give Herberling the information he'd asked for about the *Aurora*'s route. That Herberling would have to ask Hercules Maritime for that."

"There's nothing like that here. You got a copy of everything I have."

Which was puzzling, because Braithwaite had given Julie photocopies of everything he'd sent Herberling, including that message. "But Herberling's file contained that list of *Aurora*'s officers, right? As well as the one with Touchstone's name?"

"No—actually I didn't find those two papers in the file. They were in the vest pocket of his coat. He'd hung his coat on a hook, and his glasses case had pushed them down to the bottom of that pocket. The forensics team found them and gave them to me with the rest of his personal effects when they finished investigating the crime scene. I just figured they were part of the *Golden Dawn* file and included them with the papers I sent you." Mack went on more slowly, "Apparently, Bert's killer found Braithwaite's note in the file and took it. But he missed the ones in Bert's coat pocket." Then he added, "And I was dumb enough to miss their importance."

Julie was well aware that she made her share of mistakes,

too, but what counted now was correcting them. "There has to be a link between the two ships, Mack. Maybe crew qualifications. Maybe Rossi had a false officer's ticket, and that led Herberling to question the qualifications of the *Golden Dawn*'s officers. If any of them were unqualified, and if anyone in Hercules Maritime's home office knew that—Wood, say—"

"Right, Julie! It would negate their claim on the *Golden Dawn*'s loss.*"

"And suppose the officers of the *Aurora Victorious* became subject to subpoena? Suppose Rossi was called to testify that his papers were fake, or even that Hercules Maritime or Wood knew that when he signed on the *Aurora*?"

"Oh, yeah!"

Qualified maritime officers of junior rank, Julie had been told over and over, were hard to find, especially for tanker work. Yet insurance companies demanded that ships have fully certified crews in order to be covered. It was a motive. There were still big holes in the theory—the premeditation angle, for instance, and the murders of Pierce and his family. But a vague shape was emerging, and it reinforced a tie between the two ships. "What did you find out about Captain Boggs?"

"Like I said, only a little. His credit reports go back five years, to when he started with Hercules Maritime. If he had trouble before that, the records don't show it. Nothing overdue in the past five years, no loan apps at all in the last three years. Savings and checking at Barclay's, no overdrafts. House in Hampstead Heath bought three years ago and payments up to date. I don't have the price, but my London agent says there are some very nice homes in that area, and Boggs's payments are two thousand, fifty-three pounds a month. No tax liens. Plays the horses now and then at the neighborhood bookie's. No police record; not even a drunk driving charge. Two children, both grown and gone. Lives alone with his wife. When he's ashore, that is. Wife active in church. Has her own paid-up accounts at Fortnum & Mason, Clarke's, Sainsbury's, Harrow's of Northgate, and a couple other places."

"Not hurting for money, then."

"Quite comfortable. According to his taxable pay from Hercules Maritime, his house payments push him to the edge of his income. But if he has a little extra from somewhere—luck on the ponies now and then, or if his wife has money—he's not overextended."

"I thought he had been out of work for a long time."

"But no records from that time. If he was in debt, he's paid off what he owed and had the files purged."

"If I need more on Boggs, can I use your agent here?"

"Audrey Bennett. She's expensive, though."

"I'll check with my client before I get in touch with her."

Mack gave her Audrey Bennett's London number, and Julie gave him her hotel's telephone and fax numbers.

"Julie," he urged her in a quiet voice, "don't push things too hard, okay? We don't want to make it—ah—imperative for somebody to get rid of your father. And remember: He's a big lad. He can take care of himself."

"I hope so."

XVI

No one knew where the story began or how it passed from ear to ear, but within twenty-four hours the whole crew had heard of the fight between Raiford and the first mate. Pressler did not appear on the bridge for two days, the captain took over the mate's twelve-to-four watch in tight-lipped silence, and all orders from the first mate were issued by messenger. The other officers' attitudes toward Raiford shifted to cool distance. As near as he could figure, it wasn't because they were sensitive to Pressler's feelings; rather, it seemed a more general embarrassment at Raiford's doing what simply was not done. Even Li, who had been the friendliest, was guarded. Any chore that required Raiford to communicate with the first mate was relayed through Shockley. Otherwise, he was shunned at meals, in the wardroom, and at the evening cinema.

The crew, too, said nothing about it. In the presence of the other officers, the Chinese stewards and sailors even avoided looking at Raiford. Sam, who had not been seen for a couple of days after the fight, was reassigned to chip paint. Raiford glimpsed him occasionally, far down the green deck or on a platform slung over the ship's rail to dangle just above the heaving foam of the ocean.

His new assistant was Alfred, whose last name was not Wang, and he did not come from the same village where Sam and many of the crew had been recruited. In fact, Alfred's height and bulk—taller and heavier than the Taiwanese— marked him as coming from northern China. Unsmiling, he kept himself apart from the rest of the crew. Though the man understood enough English to hand him the right tools, Raiford couldn't guess how much more he spoke because he seldom said anything.

The entire ship's complement—officers and men—apparently believed Raiford had earned some kind of punishment. Pressler may have deserved what he got, but Raiford had assaulted the rigid chain of command that supported the authority of every officer and petty officer, and which ran from captain to cabin boy. It meant, ironically, that in his remaining few days aboard, he would be even less effective in finding out what happened to Rossi. He'd allowed his temper to play into the hands of those who would keep information from him, and he had only himself to blame. But he would not stand by and watch Pressler kick a helpless man. And he knew that if Pressler tried to stomp another sailor into pulp, he and the mate were going to repeat that first discussion. Raiford hoped Pressler knew it too.

The sullen ship, logging about two hundred and eighty nautical miles every twenty-four hours, steamed into the empty reaches of the Indian Ocean. But the ocean's larger waves did not make the ship roll any heavier. Rather, there was a kind of forward lurch far down in the quivering hull as if the shove of the following seas let the laboring engines rhythmically grab a breath before churning the screw once more against the sluggish weight of the cargo. Driven by a following wind, blue crests hissed close to the main deck and spilled swirls and blossoms of foam that shone glaring white against the clear cobalt depths. They raced along the hull from the stern, peaked high when they met the bow wave, broke off the blunt stem in a turbulent trough, and re-formed as a giant swell of dark and wind-chapped sea disappearing toward the wriggling line of the southern horizon.

A few days into the Indian Ocean, Raiford found himself beside Shockley on the main deck of the bridge's open promenade, enjoying the welcome shade and fresh sea wind. For a long time, both men silently watched the waves heave past the wallowing ship.

"This is the northern monsoon I heard about, right? North wind carrying us down to the Cape?"

Shockley grunted affirmative but nothing else.

During lunch, the ship's noon chit had been announced over the intercom—the knots sailed since noon yesterday, assignments to working parties and maintenance details for the afternoon, the name of the night's cinema, any birthdays among the ship's complement, and, for Muslims, the direction of Mecca. It had become the longest communication Raiford heard.

But now Shockley surprised him by clearing his throat. "First Mate wants you to run some programs this afternoon. Cargo projections. Says you're to make damn sure the results are accurate." The pudgy man no longer used Pressler's name when he passed orders on to Raiford. "Mr. Pressler" had become "First Mate," as if to emphasize Raiford's purely functional existence. "Here's the figures." He handed Raiford two slips of Teletype paper.

Each had been torn from a longer message. The figures were for two programs, one off-loading, the other on-loading. Among the first set of figures, Raiford recognized some by-now familiar data: the mathematical description of the *Aurora Victorious*'s tank capacities and its current load of Halul and Saudi crudes. The second set he did not recognize. "Planning to take a little oil out of our tanks?"

"Don't know. First Mate wants both programs tested by eight bells." Shockley disappeared into the bridge.

"Sure," said Raiford to the closing weather door. "Happy to."

The tests involved running the figures through the Lodicator, which was programmed with the *Aurora*'s capacities, then feeding the result to the Sweding machine. Its results would project the proper trim for the ship, based on a particular unloading pattern. That output would be compared to that of the ISIS 300 on the bridge. The ISIS 300 would give the navigation bridge a monitoring plan for the unloading, and Raiford's tests would indicate the range of limitations to be programmed into the ISIS alert system. The figures, complicated by dealing with two different weights of oil in adjoining holds, had been telexed from shore. Raiford guessed that someone in the home office, worried about the possibility of bad weather on either side of the Cape at this time of year, wanted to be certain the *Aurora* would unload the least amount of valuable cargo.

The home office had done the basic mathematics, and now it was up to the electronics officer to feed the new program accurately into the ship's computers and to verify the outcome before actual off-loading. In this program, the amount to jettison came to little more than three percent of the total cargo, enough to raise the ship to its winter load line. The dollar cost of dumping that much crude wasn't in the numbers Raiford had been given, but at, say seven to nine barrels a ton, and figuring for ease of arithmetic a value of, say, $100 to the barrel, the range was between $500,500 and $656,560. Compared to the value of the entire multimillion-dollar cargo, that didn't sound like much. But it did add up to a couple days' pay for a private eye, and the idea of just pumping that many dollars overboard made you swallow a time or two.

The second set of figures was for an entirely different cargo space. A penciled note in the paper's margin said "SP.2," which looked like a file's call letters. Raiford settled in front of the loading control room's terminal and tapped into the memory of the ship's computer. Scanning down the alphabetized files, he found SP.2 and tried to open it. But access was coded and the only information he could find was the time of the file's last use: May 13, 10:22 A.M. That would have been during the *Aurora*'s previous voyage, when Rossi was still aboard. And the programmer would have been the man he was replacing, Pierce.

A glance through the loading plan told him it was for a smaller tanker: the number of stress points to be monitored was almost two-thirds less than the *Aurora*'s. However, the cargo specifics matched the specific gravity of the Halul and Saudi oil now carried by the *Aurora*. Which, since Raiford was paid to think nasty thoughts, gave him an idea. But the idea that the *Aurora* would dump its excess into the smaller vessel was short-lived for a couple of reasons. While half a million dollars might be a lot of pocket change for Raiford, it would barely cover expenses for even a small tanker to cruise this far into the Indian Ocean in order to take on that oil. Second, according to the figures he had been given for loading the smaller vessel, the quantity of oil to be loaded was over three times the amount scheduled to be dumped—adding up to at least a million and a half dollars and a little change. There was no way the *Aurora Victorious* could become that light on tonnage without some very embarrassing questions from the oil company at the final delivery point. They would measure what was delivered against what the port inspector said was originally loaded. . . . Unless, of course, that inspector was part of whatever was going on. . . .

Those were some of the objections to the suspicions that had entered his mind, and they were good ones. Nonetheless, they didn't answer why the *Aurora*'s computer had in its memory a loading plan for a smaller vessel. Or why that plan had to be updated to match the type of oil in the *Aurora*'s tanks.

Raiford spent the afternoon chatting with the Lodicator as he recalculated both plans. He put in the new data, answered questions the program raised when he tinkered with its basic figures, asked the program questions when the results needed more computation. Finally, he adjusted the binomial sequences of operating commands to stay within the parameters of the new loading plans. And—as Shockley had demanded—checked and double-checked the figures for accuracy before feeding the information to the Sweding machine for its projections. Shockley, who periodically hung over Raiford's shoulder in silence, took a deep breath when the machine at last chattered its conclusions.

He studied the rows of data on the paper curling out of the printer. "Is this accurate?"

"According to the numbers you gave me. Why are we figuring the load for another ship?"

"Who says we are?"

"The program." Raiford pointed at the printout. "Those numbers aren't for the *Aurora*. They're for a smaller ship."

Shockley's ears turned dark under their suntan and he blinked rapidly as he looked hard at the paper. Finally he said, "I don't know. It was a request from shore. Probably one of the company's ships that doesn't have its own computers. A smaller ship, you say? That's it, then—a lot of smaller tankers don't have a computer of their own, so we do it for them." He hurried out of the loading room, the printouts clutched tightly in his fist.

XVII

Julie once again tried the radiophone. She suspected that whoever had isolated her father would expect her to try. So she did, with the same empty result. The captain, should he bother to answer, could tell Julie that Raiford had left the ship, that he never arrived, that he fell down a ladder, and there was no way she could challenge the man's statement. It was the same dead end Rossi's parents had hit months ago. Julie, deeply worried despite Mack's reassuring words, understood more sharply the frustration and anger that had finally driven the Rossis to hire someone to shake some kind of response out of the bland silence.

But she did know that something was going on beneath that silence, something important enough to cost the lives of four people, including a child, to protect it. And she knew that her father was targeted—unless she could stir up enough dust to draw their attention from him. And since a moving target would best attract that attention, she'd better get moving.

The after-work crowd filled Russell Square Station, queuing up at the turnstiles, squeezing onto the escalators, jamming the platforms to press toward the hissing doors of the incoming trains. Julie looked for anyone following her, but the hundreds of faces made that difficult. King's Cross Station, where she wound through tunnels and up and down stairs to the Northern line, was even more congested. The jostling throngs were not helped by buskers who clogged the passageways and whose various instruments or straining voices echoed down the tiled walls to mingle in a constant noise. The packed car surged forward, pushing her against fellow passengers who clung to the chrome rails and dangling hand-bulbs and swayed with the racketing lurch of the train. She suffered the close rub of a man whose breath heated the side of her neck and who kept trying to catch her eye as he let the crowd press his body hotly against her curves. Then, with relief, she squeezed through the doors at the Hampstead stop. Following the tide of legs and scuffling shoes up the stairs, she exited into an early evening light that nonetheless made her blink like a mole.

The taxi dropped her at the corner of Carlingsford and Worseley. As she strolled up the quiet street, she was able to keep a cautious eye behind. But no one seemed to follow. At the top of a small hill, she turned right toward Captain

Boggs's address. The homes, some brick, some half timber, many stucco, were three and four stories tall, the gardens walled with brick or fieldstone. Large enclosed verandahs were popular, as were expensive cars: Bentley, Mercedes, Jaguar, and the occasional Land Rover. Even the small convenience shops tucked away on street corners, picturesque in design and cozily understated in advertising, had the aroma of money.

Boggs Manor, a square brick building painted white and touched with Georgian motifs, rose three stories above a ground-level service floor. Each had a full-width glassed-in porch. Through the gathering twilight, the first-floor porch showed large green plants and comfortably placed wicker furniture. A carriage drive ran between the house and a high brick wall, also painted white, to the closed green doors of a two-story detached garage. The ceramic nameplate in the white brick gatepost said WILLOW HOUSE. Pale roses blown large and losing their petals to the coming winter bordered a manicured plot of grass. In the center of the garden, a large willow tree draped its soft branches in yellowing glory to justify the home's name. Julie was reminded of some of the old-money neighborhoods in American cities of the eastern seaboard—Baltimore, Norfolk, Charleston. Homes, safely anchored in neighborhoods whose wealth had defended them against decline or even change, homes that had been expensive when built and were even more expensive now. In fact, when a home like that came up for sale, it was rarely placed on the open market.

Yet Boggs had bought one of these very impressive homes. After working for Hercules Maritime for just half a dozen years, he put down a lot of money and was now keeping up with a mortgage that almost matched his pay.

Julie's shoes shuffled in the autumn leaves littering the sidewalk. Downhill and around a slight bend, a pub's genteel sign glowed warmly: the CROWN AND FEATHER. A hand-lettered notice beside the entry stated the pub hours—traditional ones, here, of course—and the mahogany and brass interior had the slow feel of just having reopened for the evening trade.

"Yes, miss?" A smiling, heavy-faced man wiped his hands on a bar cloth as he popped through swinging doors that led to the kitchen. "What's your pleasure?"

Julie ordered a shandygaff, watching the publican pull two or three times on the pump handle and drain off a half mug of foam before filling it with ginger beer. Five-pounds fifty, a price tailored to the local incomes as well as eliciting the fifty-p tip that would not be reported for tax purposes. "This is a very attractive area—very nice homes along here," she said.

"Thank you, miss—quite lovely, everyone says, and I won't argue with them. Canadian, are you?"

"American. And looking for a house to buy or rent."

"Ah, well, couldn't do better than Hampstead. Especially if you intend to work in London. Mind you, there are other nice areas. But I'm partial to this one. A very settled feel to it, miss. Comfortable, like, and quite safe for young ladies living alone."

Julie nodded. "I suppose the homes don't often go on the market?"

"Ah, as to that I couldn't say. But any estate agent could assist you. In fact, one usually stops by of an evening. Retired now, I believe, but he still knows all there is about the area. If you'd like, I can point him out when he comes in."

"That would be lovely! Please do."

"My pleasure. I have seen notices posted toward West Hampstead. Not quite up to this area, of course, but still very comfortable. Have you looked there?"

"Well, I do like being near the heath. The husband of an acquaintance bought a home just up the street a couple of years ago. She has nothing but high praise for the neighborhood."

"Well, there you are: they do come up for sale now and then."

"I suspect they were very fortunate. His name is Boggs— a sea captain. Lives at Willow House. This must be the pub they've spoken of. His wife said they've spent some very pleasant evenings here."

"Ah, thank you, miss. That's lovely to hear. Boggs . . . Boggs . . . Willow House . . . sea captain . . ." Julie guessed that the man's off-season trade was primarily neighborhood residents and his success depended on his ability to recall their names. "Yes—tall chap, I believe. Rather thin. Thought there was something of the military about him. Each December, for a week or two, he and his missus dine here a number of times. Then they're off to their finca in Spain. Sea captain, eh? That tells me why we don't see him the rest of the year, don't it?"

"Captain of an oil tanker. He's done quite well. Must, to afford Willow House."

"Indeed. Lovely home, that."

"And another house in Spain? A finca, you say?"

"Near Alicante, it is. My wife and I make our pilgrimage to Majorca every January, and I remember talking with the Boggses about Alicante. Very nice home, from what his missus mentioned. Overlooking the sea. Private bit of beach. Away from the usual tourist haunts."

The early trade began to drift in. The publican excused himself to greet and serve. The barstools and small booths began to hold a smattering of men in their fifties and older. Wearing casual but expensive tweed, they spoke quietly together or exchanged a friendly word with the publican and then drank alone. Their eyes occasionally drifted toward Julie in cautious assessment. None of them, Julie supposed, had exchanged names with anyone else when they first started coming here twenty or thirty years ago, and they still weren't about to invade one another's privacy without a proper introduction. Like cats, they seemed at home in their favorite corner, and their animal comfort lent contentment to the room. Near the fireplace with its flickering gas log was the dining area. Another sign in hand-lettered script indicated a family room and patio in the rear—where children would be welcome. Beside the fireplace, a chalkboard listed the day's menu. A portly woman in her forties—probably the bartender's wife—took dinner orders and gave directions to two young, overworked girls who hurried to do the serving and bussing.

Julie sipped a second glass—a detective's lot didn't always have to be an unhappy one, even at five pounds per drink— and was finally introduced by the publican to an elderly, tweed-coated gentleman who said his name was Andrew and that he would be delighted to talk about local estate properties, or, really, anything else she wished to discuss. A wrinkled hand lifted its glass of whiskey in a chivalric toast to Julie, and Andrew settled onto the booth's other bench.

"Willow House?" Andrew's frayed white mustache stretched in a wide smile. "Yes, of course! Belonged to the Brierlies for a number of years. Always liked that: Brierlies and Willows. Two different species of plant, eh? Strikes one as droll, eh? Smythe-Rogers before that—no pun there at all. Oakley. Now that would be a good one: Oakley and Willow, eh? What's that? Price? Price and Willow . . . ? Don't really see . . . Oh, you mean price of the house! It would be up there. All the homes around here cost a pretty penny and go up in value every year. Damned labor government. Haven't met your Captain Boggs. Boggs and Willow—Willow Boggs! Might make something of that, eh? But Brierlie wasn't one to sell a cow for a calf—knew the value of his property, he did. If your Captain Boggs paid his price, he paid a-plenty. Wouldn't do otherwise, would it? Values go down, blacks move in, neighborhood goes to ruin. Can't have things end up like East London, eh? No doubt your Captain Boggs could sell it tomorrow for more than he paid, but he'd have the devil's own time buying another. Unless he had the cash, of course, and didn't mind parting with it. Always someone's got the eye out for a good profit—discreet inquiries only, you understand. No one wants it known that they must sell. Don't know of one right off, though. Might ask Mellers—he was the estate agent transacted the Brierlie sale, I believe. Yes. Mellers. Offices in Hampstead—should be in the directory, eh? It's the man's job to be located, eh? Mellers—sellers, a bit droll, eh?"

When Julie finally left the pub, the chill night air cleared her smoke-stung eyes and made her wish for one of the heavy knit sweaters that a number of the pub's customers wore. The lights of the large homes were hidden behind shrubbery and walls, and scattered streetlamps only intensified the darkness. London's high latitude—level with the southern tip of Hudson's Bay—meant that autumn nights came early and, despite the Gulf Stream that blessed the land, cold. In a sky clear of the day's haze, the northern constellations looked hard and bright and close. The giant W of Cassiopeia's Chair and the tiny North Star it circled were almost overhead. Julie took a moment from her brisk stride and her thoughts about Boggs to admire the icy glitter of the sharply etched stars.

And that was when she was hit.

A squeaking whisper of rubber soles warned her an instant before the black shape exploded at the side of her vision. Reflexively, she pulled back, feeling more than seeing the blur of a dark arm whip toward her face. A tug at the sleeve of her light jacket, a burning sting along her forearm. The dim gray of pavement showed the shadow of legs and Julie dropped to her unwounded arm to scissor her feet hard and catch a knee between her swinging heel and toe.

A grunt as the vague shape fell awkwardly and Julie rolled away, her momentum carrying her over her own shoulder and up to her feet to face what she now saw was a scrambling figure dressed in black with a black cloth covering its face. In front of that cloth, the hard glitter of a stiletto wove back and forth like a snake's head. She aimed a hard kick at his groin but he was expecting that and hopped back.

Her eye on the steely gleam, Julie moved sideways from the knife, forcing the man to attack across his body. The arm struck out and Julie grabbed behind the blade, her fingernails digging into a wrist as she thudded the heel of her other hand savagely against the back of an elbow.

"Gawd—!"

The hairy wrist twisted from Julie's grasp. The blade whistled sharply past her ear in a vicious swipe at her throat.

Desperately, Julie kicked out. The side of her shoe caught something solid that sent the shape stumbling back into the street. Julie, arm now burning deeply, gasped for breath and moved in again, searching the blackness for the flicker of the knife.

A flash of automobile lights swung uphill behind her. Their glare showed the black gloves covering his hands, the black balaclava over his face, and his eyes momentarily blinking against the headlights. Julie lunged, one hand ready to deflect the knife, the other aiming at the glint of eyes. But the man turned and ran into the dark past the rapidly approaching car.

Julie staggered back onto the sidewalk as the vehicle swerved to miss her. The dim glimmer of a face, smudges of wide eyes, a gaping mouth turned toward her. Then the car accelerated in fright up the hill. In the silence, Julie crouched and listened and searched the dark. The only sounds were her own heavy breath and, somewhere toward the lightless expanse of the heath, the distant rustle of busy vehicle traffic. On her forearm, she felt the spreading fire of cold air on gaping flesh, as well as the tickle of blood. It seemed as if Julie's ploy of distracting attention from her father was working—better and more quickly than she had planned.

XVIII

Raiford no longer took his coffee in the wardroom. After supper, he helped himself to a soda pop from the vending machine on the main deck and carried it up to his quarters where he read until he finally dropped off to sleep. So it was a surprise, after several nights, to hear a scratch on his door. At first he thought the faint noise was at a neighboring cabin. But it came again, and, shrugging on one of the ship's heavy bathrobes, he unlocked the door.

"Mr. Raifah—your coffee, sah." The deck steward held a covered tray on his shoulder, face impassive.

Understanding, he stepped back so the man could carry the tray in. "Took you long enough, Woody," he said loudly as he closed the door.

It really was coffee, and the steward busied himself serving as he spoke quietly. "Sam is very sorry for the trouble he makes for you, Mr. Raifah. He wants me to tell you."

"He didn't make the trouble, Woody." His voice, too, was low. The uninsulated steel bulkheads between cabins carried sound easily and were the cause of occasional witticisms by neighbors of officers whose wives had come aboard.

"His fault, he says. Very sorry." Woody clattered the cup and saucer loudly over the murmur of his voice. "First Mate kick him very hard. Very . . ." He searched for the word, eyes turning toward the cciling for inspiration. "Hurt—skin all dark."

"Bruised?"

"Bruise—yes. Very bruise. Any more kicks maybe break something and he cannot work no more. Sam say thank you very much."

"Tell him I hope he's feeling all right now. That sort of thing happen a lot?"

"Sometimes. Depends. Sometimes First Mate very angry alla time. Sometimes not. Nobody likes him. You are a good man, not same as him." Woody frowned as he poured the coffee, eyes on the smoking stream. "First Mate is very dangerous. You please be careful, sah."

"Is that what happened to Mr. Rossi? He had a fight with the First Mate?"

"No. He fall overboard."

"Was another ship alongside when he fell?"

"Oh, yes. Little tanker. Mr. Rossi reach way out for line to secure hose. Too far. Fall down between." The man's slender hand made a rolling motion. "I see him—call 'man over- board.' First Mate tells me shut up and we leave Mr. Rossi. First Mate says keep off-loading—keep working. Never mind Mr. Rossi."

"He was still alive and they didn't stop for him?"

"Yes. Mr. Rossi wave his arms, try to swim." Woody clat- tered his silver-plated serving dishes together so that Raiford barely heard his words. "Leave him sink behind ship."

Raiford sighed a long breath. Then he murmured, "What happened to Rossi's personal effects? Letters or clothes or other gear?"

"In his footlocker, sah."

"What happened to it?"

Woody shrugged. "Maybe went to slop chest."

"Everything?"

He bobbed his head and shuffled nervously. "Man die, all the good stuff goes to the slop chest. Cheaper than send it home—makes money for ship's store, too." He added, "Rest of his stuff . . ." and ended in a shrug.

Raiford could be wearing Rossi's plimsoles.

"I must go—Mr. Raifah, you be very careful, please. First Mate your enemy now. Much danger for you."

"I will, Woody. Thanks." Raiford leaned into the passage- way to call after the tinkling tray, "And next time don't take so damned long getting here—I like my coffee hot!"

Silent, but ready to hand any tool needed, Alfred stood at Rai- ford's side. Much of the electronics work did not require an assistant, and given the small number of crewmen, it seemed Alfred could have served better chipping paint or helping with the ceaseless maintenance in the engine room. But the sailor was less aide than guard, and the man's presence kept other crewmen from talking to Raiford.

Today's schedule called for a calibration check of the temperature sensors, those that monitored each section of the old boilers as well as those watching over the condenser and turbine. The lower levels of the engine room, dim with spotty lighting and intricate shadows, were hot and damp with steam. It was here that Raiford's claustrophobic dislike of ships grew intense, and here that the age of the *Aurora* was most evident. Steam leaked in tiny plumes around valves and fittings crusted with years of mineral deposits or slick with beards of slimy brown rust. The second engineering officer, Henderson, had told Raiford that the ship was one of the few still powered by steam rather than diesel engines, and its age forced them to lie idle for a day every three months so the accumulating leaks could be tightened up. "If we didn't, we'd lose our steam and the old tub would up and die. Steam runs everything: steerage, electricity, your precious computers, pumps and loading systems, everything. Not so bad if it comes when we're in port waiting to load. Damned expensive at sea. Lose a good fifteen or twenty hours at over five thousand dollars a day." He added, "Then the captain pushes her at flank speed to make up the bleeding time and that starts the leaks all over again."

Water distillation was another nagging problem for the

engineering officer. The steam leaks, though small, added up to a loss of thirty tons of distilled water a day. The evaporation unit produced freshly distilled replacement water at only thirty-five tons. A five-ton margin was, Henderson said, almost no margin at all. The large boiler making the steam that turned the turbine and its single massive propeller shaft used distilled water that had to be absolutely clean. Impurities would dry and cake against the boiler's steel wall and cause uneven heat. The resultant hot spots could burn through the side of the boiler in a matter of hours, and that made the heat sensors and Raiford's job all the more vital.

"As for the condenser, don't ask."

Raiford promised he wouldn't, but Henderson wanted him to understand how important maintenance duties were. The condenser was a pipe system that cooled the steam back into water after it had run through the turbine. "Has to be water when it goes into the boiler, right? Otherwise, the fire burns through the bottom just like your granny's teapot when it's empty." Seawater, used for cooling the condenser, was drawn in through the ship's hull, circulated around the steam pipes in the condenser chamber. Then the seawater was pumped out in a steady warm stream above the waterline. But seawater corrodes metal, and old metal corrodes faster, and the engineering officers had a constant battle to keep the cooling seawater from leaking into the condenser's steam pipes and contaminating the pure water used for the engine. "Another reason why the heat sensors are so important, right? Warning light on the monitor board lets us know if the bloody condenser unit's sprung another leak. Gives us a chance to shut down and patch up before any harm's done to the boiler."

As Raiford and Alfred worked their way down a narrow catwalk along the shuddering flanks of the towering boiler, the clank of tools and high-pitched voices cut through the humming throb of burners and pumps, turbine and screw. A glare of bright light from the level below showed the engineering shop where three crewmen stood pounding at a length of pipe clamped in the vises of a metal worktable. One was Sam, who, glancing up, stared for a long moment through the grill of the catwalk toward Raiford and then turned quickly back to his work. The voices dropped beneath the engine room's rumble. Raiford tested the readings of sensor fourteen and, squinting against the fiery glare and heat spilling from a small vision port, recorded the test date on its inspection tag. Then he moved to the next unit. At number eighteen, he shook his flashlight and thumped it against the heel of his hand.

"Alfred, me lad—the electric torch is out. Can't read the meter. Go up to ship's stores and trade these for new batteries." He tilted the flashlight over the man's hand and let its batteries slide into the open palm. "Just like these, got it? Battery—electric torch—chop chop. Got it?"

The man's black eyes narrowed slightly and he nodded once. Raiford watched through the steamy air as the dark coveralls flickered away in the patches of light along the catwalk. When Alfred was out of sight, Raiford swung quickly down a ladder way toward the three seamen.

Sam saw him first. A startled look crossed his face. He

peered past Raiford then scanned the catwalk along the tall side of the boiler. When he did not see Alfred, Sam smiled widely, "Mr. Raifah—thank you! Thank you!"

"How you feeling, Sam? Everything okay?"

"Everything okay—and you, Mr. Raifah—you are treated very bad now, yes? Very sorry," he said, still grinning.

The other two sailors grinned just as widely. Raiford shook his head. "No problem. Woody told me to be careful. He also said things could get dangerous. What did he mean, Sam? What kind of things?"

The smile went away and the man wagged his head. "Tanker work is very dangerous alla time. Alla time work very fast—hurry alla time." Another wag. "First Mate maybe gives you work so you have accident, yes? That Alfred is not good man—works for First Mate, yes? When he works along with you, you look out for him."

"Thanks, Sam. Will do."

A clanging noise echoed faintly through the noise. Sam, frightened, looked up toward the catwalk and said hurriedly, "You meet me at the fantail, four bells tonight, yes?"

"Right—see you then." Raiford scrambled back up the ladder. Alfred, a gliding wedge of darkness in the steam, flickered toward him.

"Batteries." He handed them to Raiford, eyes studying the taller man, then the three sailors working industriously below.

"Right." Raiford dropped them into the L-shaped flashlight. "Let's get this over with. I'm starting to get moldy."

Muted by the hiss of waves and the hum of wind across struts and cables, the ship's bell came softly from the intercom. The stern was a vast black shadow whose taffrail and butts, winches, drums, and hawseholes were silhouetted against the wide band of churned sea that unrolled like a faintly glowing ribbon into the darkness. Gleams of pale green flickered and surged beyond the ship's flanks as phosphorescent waves broke into foam under the steady push of the northern monsoon. Above, towering into a moonless sky filled with more stars than Raiford had seen in a long time, the aft face of the ship's island gleamed here and there with uncurtained windows. Yet, despite its size, the island was but a small focus of life and light in a darkness that stretched forever.

Four bells of the third watch. Most of the officers and ratings would be in the crew's mess watching the evening movie, an old Charles Bronson film called *Messenger of Death*. For some reason, Bronson was a favorite with the crew. But Raiford had seen this dog on late-night television and didn't feel he was missing anything now. Nor would his fellow officers miss him—they had come to expect his absence.

High in the stars overhead, the wind made a hollow sound across the ship's funnel. Raiford's eyes, grown accustomed to the dark in the twenty minutes he had been waiting, made out the trail of quickly blown smoke that blotted and dimmed stars over the port bow. He hunched deeper into his jacket. With the equatorial sun gone, even a sea wind as warm as this one felt chill. Leaning into the shelter of the lifeboat, he waited.

Finally, a vague figure moved quickly against the pale bridge. A moment later, the shape reappeared against the sea's glow. It stood motionless for a breath or two and then gingerly came forward.

Raiford stepped out of the shadow of the lifeboat davit. "How're you doing, Sam?"

A sharp intake of breath followed by a relieved sigh. "Ah—Mr. Raifah!" Sam stepped close, bringing the thick odor of garlic from the evening meal. "Very dark here. You wait long?"

"Long enough to be sure we're alone. What do you want to tell me?"

Sam's voice, tensely muted, spewed as if a plug had been pulled. "Ah, Mr. Raifah, this is a very bad ship—very bad! Treat sailors very bad—take too much pay for everything: movies, crimp, laundry, even TV. So much they take out! Even take money for safety class—must go to safety class every week and pay for class. And First Mate very bad. All the time he hits sailors, calling them names. That Alfred very bad. Works for First Mate. Spies on crew. Tells First Mate to fire this man, give that man hard work or dangerous work—"

"Well, go to another ship. Can't you move to another ship?"

"No—crimp say I must work here. He keeps much pay until my contract is finished. Three years. If I leave ship early, no pay, no repat."

"I don't know what to tell—"

"Very dangerous work this tanker. Now is more dangerous

with new Plimsoll. Work very much overtime and no pay for it—not enough crew for all the work—too little sailors for keeping ship to run . . ."

Sam's English was a lot better than Raiford's Chinese, but it was breaking down under the pressure of his complaints. Raiford had trouble understanding the tumbling words whose syllables began to separate and take on the rise and fall of his native language. "Whoa, Sam—slow down. What do you mean, a new Plimsoll?"

"New Plimsoll. Plimsoll line. New paint. Makes ship curry more but looks same."

"You mean you painted over the old Plimsoll line with a new one?"

"Not new one over old one. Black paint over old Plimsoll and new Plimsoll higher up side. Ship carries more oil but new Plimsoll looks okay to inspectors."

"This ship is overloaded?"

"Yes! Big overload. Very dangerous. Ship very easy to break up now. Easy to sink in storm. Very dangerous now and sailors very frightened."

"How much overloaded?"

A shadowy shrug and a wide stretch of both arms.

"You moved the Plimsoll line up that far?"

"More."

"More? When was this done?"

"Three—maybe four voyages. Clean tanks, move Plimsoll up. Very lucky so far no big storms. But dangerous, too—a big storm is coming some time."

"You've gone around the Cape in July and August with the overload?"

"No—no. Not around the Cape. Off-load to another tanker before the Cape."

"Did Mr. Rossi know about this?"

Another shrug. "Officer."

Sam had more complaints on his list, most of which Raiford could make out: the chief steward took kickbacks from crewmen for assigning good jobs; the new third officer, Li, was from Mainland China and didn't like Taiwanese; the crewmen weren't allowed to go ashore at any port until the three-year contract was up; sickness or injury meant docked pay or abandonment; Captain Boggs never listened to crew complaints; one man who tried to complain, a long time ago, was beaten so badly by Pressler that he had been left ashore in St. Croix.

"How much do you get paid?"

"Very good pay: bunk, food, and thirty dollars every month." The shadowy hands waved helplessly. "But only ten dollars a month goes home. Ship's fees and crimp take alla rest."

Raiford felt a mixture of guilt, anger, and depression. Guilt because as an officer he was treated like a human while these men were exploited like animals. Anger at the greed and contempt the vessel's owners had for those who risked their lives serving the owners' profit. Depression because there wasn't much he could do about changing a system where the seamen had no justice to appeal to, no representation with the ship's owners. They came from a part of the world where others would quickly and gratefully take their places.

"I'll try to think of something, Sam. I don't know what I can do to help you out, but I'll try."

Later in his cabin, listening to the silence of the deeply laden vessel and feeling the rhythmic, gentle tremor of the bulkheads as the ship surged through pushing seas, Raiford's mind was divided between Sam's plea for help—"Mr. Raifah, you are a good man. You can help sailors, yes?"—and the implications of the overloaded tanks. The latter point was his job, but the stories of unfair treatment kept breaking into his concentration. He again saw Pressler's shoe slam into Sam writhing on the deck. There should be something he could do, some way of helping these men at least get the little money they earned. But whatever it was—if it was—would have to come second.

Gradually, his anger settled and he could work through the implications of the new Plimsoll line. Using what he remembered of the data programmed into the Lodicator, Raiford made a few estimates of tonnage—volume, weight, and value. The rough sum his pencil came up with explained a lot. Instead of dumping around eight hundred tons of oil for a paltry value of, say, $405,000, the inclusion of the secret overload might triple the amount of oil off-loaded. In fact, he bet that new amount would be as much as twenty-seven thousand tons: the capacity of the smaller tanker he had programmed earlier. Figure nine barrels per ton at . . . again, call it $100 a barrel for easy arithmetic . . . that came to . . . $24,300,000! Raiford carefully refigured his calculations and then went through the math again, counting zeros and commas one more time. At a bare minimum of six barrels per ton, it came to $16,200,000. Even to a big spender like Raiford, that was a hell of a lot of money—enough to make St. Sebastian join the archery club! At $150 a barrel, it would be half again as much! And if the oil went to a port in China or Japan, the Asian surcharge would bring in even more millions. From what Sam said, the Plimsoll mark had been moved three or four voyages ago. Call it three offloads in the last year and a half, and it added up to at least forty-eight to seventy-two million dollars. If the port inspector in the Persian Gulf was paid off—and Raiford figured there was enough spare change for that purpose—then the only record of the stolen oil would be in any logbook kept by the captain of that second vessel. Which, if offered for any official inspection, could be doctored or the inspector bought. That left the only hard evidence of the larceny to be a crewman willing to testify to a midsea transfer. Raiford could guess what the life expectancy of that crewman might be.

XIX

"Nasty cut."

The glare of the examining light struck deep into the sliced and gaping flesh of Julie's forearm. It showed a pink-and-white tangle like a fresh slab of marbled, raw beef. But there was surprisingly little blood.

The Pakistani doctor straightened from his inspection of her arm. "Went lengthwise down the muscle, didn't it? Just missed the nerves and veins and arteries—you were most fortunate there, miss. Not as deep as the bone, but it will require sutures rather than clamps. It's going to leave something of a scar. But I must say, you certainly did a neat job. Use a scalpel?"

"No. It was an accident."

"Oh? What kind?"

"I slipped and fell on a broken bottle."

"Really?" The doctor was about her father's age, but his dark face was lined with the weariness of long tours in the emergency ward. "Seems to have the appearance of a knife wound." He waited, but Julie added nothing. "Well, since it isn't, there's little sense bothering with a police report, eh?"

That was Julie's idea. She nodded and tried not to wince at the soreness in her neck and back.

The doctor finished sewing, painting, wrapping, and needling. "Tetanus injection should suffice. But keep an eye on the wound for any infection, yes? Swelling, redness, fever. Have a doctor look at it again within twenty-four hours." He added, "As for scar tissue, I did the best I could. But here's a salve that might reduce scarring. And you may wish to consult with a cosmetic surgeon at your earliest convenience."

Julie promised she would follow his directions, and thanked the man, who told her to stay away from broken bottles.

Despite the sedative, Julie slept restlessly. She woke every time she rolled on her arm or tangled its soreness in the sheets. Her mind was equally restless, churning in fragments and threads that kept her from easily falling back to sleep. Disjointed thoughts raised questions whose answers seemed to hover just beyond perception. Finally, in late morning, she pried her aching body out of bed and unwrapped her arm.

The long, puckering seam and the twin puncture marks of stitches were crusted with dried blood. The surrounding flesh was warm and pink with fever. But there was no red streak of blood poisoning up her arm, and the clamped lips of tender flesh looked clean of sepsis.

Gingerly holding the wound away from the shower spray, she soaked her bruised and tight muscles in hot water and toweled awkwardly. Then she washed the cut with hydrogen peroxide before wrapping it with a fresh bandage. She managed to pull a thin sweater's long sleeve over the arm. Her late breakfast was light on food but heavy on coffee.

Glancing at her watch, she placed an overseas call to Mr. Rossi, person-to-person. The man wanted to know everything that Touchstone had found out.

"There's something going on that I think involves a lot of illegal money, Mr. Rossi." She told about the deaths of the Pierce family and waited while Rossi expressed his shock. "I don't know if their deaths, Herberling's and your son's, are related. All I can say is the case is becoming very complex. I'd like your permission to hire a local agent who has more contacts in London than I do."

"Like I said before, I want to get to the bottom of Hal's death. My God, if he was murdered like those poor people—!" Rossi let silence finish his thought. "I don't give a damn what it costs. If some son of a bitch killed my boy, I want him found and hung!"

But if Harold, whose mate's license appeared to be false, had been involved in the scam . . . ? Well, she would deal with that if it came up. "All right, Mr. Rossi. I'll be in touch again as soon as possible."

Her next call was local, and the woman's voice, in lilting Jamaican, told Julie how to get to her office.

"And how is Stanley Mack doing now?" Audrey Bennett, proprietor of Bennett Services, Ltd., poured a cup of very dark tea for each of them and led Julie to the social side of the large, open loft. Her desk, computer, and telephone complex were arranged in a deep bay whose sixth-floor windows overlooked the canyon of busy Oxford Street. Julie glimpsed, past the pigeon-smeared cupolas of a gray building across the wide avenue, the spreading greenness of a corner of Hyde Park.

Audrey Bennett was short, fat, and self-possessed. A wide, white smile dominated a plain dark face. She was also, Mack had told Julie, one of the sharpest documents investigators in the world's insurance industry and did freelance work for some of the highest-paid solicitors in Britain.

"Fine. He sends his greetings. Asked me to tell you that he'll be visiting Jamaica in February and wants you to run away with him."

"Ha! 'Take her to Jamaica,' eh? He will never move from New York. He talks all the time about moving out of that city, but he will stay forever in New York." Across the room, the telephone gave a single muted ring and her tape recorder switched on with a soft click.

"Do you want to get that?"

"No. Never mind the telephone—it never stops its ringing. And if I answer all the time, people will think I never work, ha!" She swung her pink slippers onto an ottoman that anchored a Persian rug. The rug's age and size, its spongy softness, the intricacy and precision of its design and color, made Julie think it could well be a museum piece.

"You are a pretty woman with a problem. Tell me what that problem is."

Julie told her.

The part of the room they occupied was furnished in a Victorian style that, despite its ornateness, managed to be both cozy and relaxing: padded and very comfortable needlepoint chairs, a large Tiffany lamp with colors whose purity vouched for its authenticity, an electric fire rising and falling behind the isinglass of a filigreed metal fireplace. On the round table—ebony or aged oak—at Audrey's elbow, a large teapot covered with a quilted warmer sat on a white doily. It was flanked by tall porcelain cream and sugar bowls bearing tiny pink flowers that also had the look of genuine and expensive antiques.

When Julie finished, Audrey Bennett nodded. "Well, Mellers the estate agent should be no problem: a ring on the telephone. This captain would be the same captain that Stanley asked me for a financial on last week. I have done his credit history already. But his bank statements, now—" Her shoulders lifted and fell and she rubbed thumb and finger together. "That may cost a bit."

"Our client is willing to pay."

"That is the client to have."

"And your time, of course."

"Of course! Otherwise, how can I afford my Victorian splendor? But it will not be too much." She smiled whitely.

"Enjoy your tea, Miss Campbell, and watch this woman work!"

Shuffling her pink slippers into the office area, she rattled the computer keyboard to scroll a list of names and telephone numbers down the screen. Opening an entry, she punched a few more keys, and then lifted the telephone to talk. "Henry Mellers, please. It is Audrey Bennett telephoning."

The Jamaican dialect disappeared and her voice now had the rounded vowels and half-swallowed final *R*s of the Uppah Clahss. Her questions were short and almost curt; the answers she received were long, detailed, and apparently respectful. As she listened, she jotted notes on an electronic notebook, and then printed out the results for Julie. "Would you like another cuppa?"

The sheet listed the credit information that the estate agency had gathered on Boggs. The man worked as a ship's officer, rising to captain just before being made redundant. He subsequently sold his home at 85 Worsely Place, Staines, Surrey, moving to a rented flat on St. John's Road in Lambeth where he declared bankruptcy. He listed his debts as 19,308 pounds sterling and 14 pence. No assets. Later employed by Hercules Maritime, he began paying his creditors at the rate of 50 pounds per month. Maintained same rate until two years ago when he cleared bankruptcy by paying the remaining total with a lump sum of 15,108 pounds plus those 14 pence, and cleared his credit rating. A few months later, he contracted to purchase Willow House, Hampstead. The down payment was 75,000 pounds, 5,000 of which was nonrefundable and to be paid on signing. The balance—70,000 pounds sterling—was deposited in full three months after signing. The remaining cost would be met by a scheme of monthly payments from a sealed account located at the Greater Atlantic Savings and Loan, Bahamas, W.I. All payments so far had been on time.

Audrey poured them both another cup of the fragrant, hot tea. "If all your suspects get this rich this rapidly, perhaps I should have you investigate me."

Julie gave a long sigh. "He's not just a simple old sea dog, is he?"

"That bank, you know, is one of those famous offshore institutions for rich people to hide money from the tax man. We can find out some things about the account but it will cost a great deal, and any source will want anonymity." She added, "That means anything we do discover will be hearsay—not admissible evidence."

Julie nodded. A sealed account in an offshore bank, a home whose taxes and payments equaled his monthly salary, a finca in Spain. The good captain had come a long way from bankruptcy in a short time.

She had a lot more to do, but at least she now had a direction to take. "Here's another list. Officers on the *Aurora Victorious* and their home addresses. I'd appreciate the same kind of report on them, too."

"Certainly." Audrey glanced down the list. "Who is this Dorothy Fleenor? This Olivia Minkey? They have women officers on the ship?"

"No. The first is an underwriter for Marine Carriers Worldwide. The other is the widow of the captain of the MV *Golden Dawn.*"

"Oh?" She studied Julie's face for a moment. "Interesting things are going on inside that pretty head of yours, eh?"

"Just looking at a wide range of possibilities. I'm afraid there's some urgency. How long will this take?"

"This many names, maybe two days. Okay?"

"No quicker? I'm worried about my . . . partner."

Audrey shook her head. "I can try. That's all."

Another two days. Her father could take care of himself for that long. He really could. And that would give Julie's arm time to get over its soreness and the rest of her to get copies of the files from Hercules's home office. Besides, there was nothing she could do to hurry the woman. "Okay."

XX

The single beep of his alarm clock woke him at 02:00. In the dark room, he dressed and listened to the sounds of the ship. Something was different—not in the hiss of the ventilation system or the tremor of the steel bulkhead. It was in the fundamental rhythm of the entire ship. Under his bare feet, the gentle sway of the carpeted deck had also changed; the pitching motion was slower now and seemed to include a slight sideways roll as if the waves came at the ship from a new angle.

Squeezing on the canvas shoes that, without their laces, almost fit, he muffled the sound of his door lock with a folded washcloth. In the passageway a row of dim lights showed the white paint of walls and ceiling, the vacant dark carpet, the closed weather doors at each end that led to small outside wings. Through their portholes was only blackness. Alert for sounds, Raiford went swiftly to the lower bridge deck. Pausing again to listen before he pressed open the wardroom door, he softly closed it behind him. The only lighting in the empty room was a night lamp turned low. A dot of orange glare said the coffeepot stood ready for service at any time.

Raiford settled in front of the Inmarsat terminal and groped around for its telephone. Nothing. The handset was gone. Where it usually rested, a pair of empty chrome forks smiled at him. He peered into the darkness behind the machine, but neither wire nor handset rested there. Running his hands along the sides of the metal housing, his fingers stumbled on a missing panel and he tilted the heavy box to bring the cavity into the dim light. Where the cord for the handset was supposed to enter the terminal, the bright and cheery colors of disconnected wires dangled loose. The small brass slots for the shoe connectors were shiny with the scratches of recent wear: the handset had been taken out and replaced several times. Raiford guessed those times that it was replaced were at night and the purpose of taking it out was to cut off unmonitored communications from the ship.

The services of a temporary electronics officer were still needed, but the captain and first mate wanted to keep that officer incommunicado. And that hinted what would happen when they no longer needed Raiford's expertise. What it didn't tell him was exactly when that would be. Nor how he could get his information about the smaller tanker to Julie or Mack.

He sat in the half-light and considered the possibilities. His cell phone was of no use. The shortwave radio was monitored continuously on the bridge; any use of that would be heard immediately by the officer on duty and—if necessary—cut off. Same for the ship's fax and the telex. . . . Taking the Inmarsat's handset was a good move . . . an effective one, unless . . .

He stared into the darkness, tracing in his mind the relays, transmitters, connectors, and wiring diagrams. Voice or computer, it was all electrical impulses. The *Aurora* had its own modem . . . the ship's computer had a built-in modem somewhere. . . . It, too, would be monitored. But the ship's e-mail messages went out three times a day, and one of those times— a satellite connection at cheaper, off-peak hours to save the company money—was due in half an hour. The trick would be to put a message in the queue unnoticed. All e-mails were relayed through a server at Hercules Maritime. But maybe they wouldn't be screened if there were no alert. Eventually, the message log would be read over by the home office for the purpose of billing individual users, but by then it would be too late.

How . . . ? Raiford closed his eyes to see better his memory of the ship's wiring diagrams. The backup unit. The *Aurora* was an old vessel. It had a half-duplex transmitter for a backup unit. Its messages only went one way at a time, and that's where the gamble would be. But if he could patch through to that half-duplex transmitter . . .

Raiford headed belowdecks for the loading control room. He didn't know if what he had in mind would work. There were few reasons why it should, and many why it should not. But all he had was a gamble, and he'd better take it—time was passing quickly.

Easing the door shut, he tucked his shirt along its bottom crack before turning on the control room lights. The wall of dials, indicator lights, readouts, and gauges was silent and cold. At the end, anchored to its metal shelf, sat the slave-terminal that provided access to the ship's main computer. Glancing at his watch, he turned it on and punched in codes that took him deeper into the programming menus. Keys rattling swiftly, he tried first one track, then another, tracing out sequences to dead ends. Finally he found the series that led to the ship's off-board communications system. Intent, aware of passing time, he studied the numbers and symbols that filled the screen. Gradually—too gradually—with gaps, guesses, and luck, patterns fell into place and he began to read the strings of programming language. There it was: a connecting sequence to a cellular-ready modem. And it had a configuration almost identical to one he was familiar with—an old RJ-14 unit manufactured by Multi-Tech. It worked the same way as many commercial air-liners that had modems available for passengers who wanted to tap into the Internet while in flight. And, yes, he could trans-mit through the unused half-duplex. But the ship's scheduled transmission time was coming up fast. With luck, the officer on the bridge wouldn't notice an extra e-mail going out. But he needed more luck to time the transmissions. Dial the Internet . . . pause for the connection. No screen to show a reply—not with a half-duplex. Five seconds. Ten . . . twenty—that should do it. He hoped that did it. Access code . . . account number . . . personal code . . . address. Each one-way transmission required him to wait until he thought his message was acknowledged. He hoped the responses were timed right. Timing was important. He forced himself to let the second hand on his watch swing around the dial. Then he entered a long message, typing quickly to make the deadline for the ship's e-mail transmission now just minutes away: the story of the *Aurora*'s overload, the rendezvous at sea, a description of the smaller tanker's dimensions, the amount of money involved. "The functions for the loading programs come from Hercules's home office, so someone there is in on it too. I don't know if Rossi died accidentally or was killed, but it happened out of their approved sea-lane at the rendezvous, and that's why they had to be vague about the cause and especially the place of his death." He glanced at his watch again and hurried to finish, "Julie, I hope you get this. I think they're on to me, but don't worry. Things are under control."

He typed in the code for "send." There was no confirmation—the ship's e-mail could not talk back to the half-duplex. But his message should queue with the other e-mails waiting for satellite time. He hoped. And that deadline—23:35 GMT—was right about now: 02:35 local time.

Sighing, Raiford sagged against the creaking chair. His message would either go out on schedule among all the others, or it wouldn't. There was nothing he could do now except wipe the sweat from his face and keep hoping.

XXI

Raiford felt something in the air at breakfast: an edginess, a preoccupied silence among the deck officers gulping their porridge and kippers, their eggs, toast, and coffee. It was more than the usual shunning of him; rather, it was something that seemed within each of the officers and that, for the most part, did not include Raiford.

The exception was the first mate. Once, Raiford looked up to catch Pressler staring at him. Above the corner of the man's tight mouth a fresh, maroon scar creased the flesh. Hatred made the man's eyes hard, and his muscular shoulders were tensed around his neck.

Raiford grinned and offered to pass the Thermos pot. "Care for a cuppa?"

The mate whipped his face away, the side of his thick neck

turning dark red. No one at the long table lifted eyes from their plates. Shockley, who had been stuffing down a large bowl of porridge, suddenly seemed to lose his appetite and stared blankly at the tablecloth. Then he blinked and looked up. His eyes touched on Raiford and then jerked away. He wiped his mouth and shoved his chair back.

"Duty calls." His voice was hoarse and no one replied.

Raiford was last to leave the table. Johnny bustled around while the steward cleared the dishes. Shockley had not yet passed on to Raiford the first mate's orders for the day. The absence of a duty station felt odd, as if, already shunned, Raiford had now become invisible as well.

In the empty passageway, he half listened to the clatter of dishes in the dining saloon and felt another subtle shift in the *Aurora*'s pulse. Up in his quarters, he was staring out his window at the long stretch of vacant green deck when he heard a key in his lock.

"Come in."

"Oh—very sorry!" The deck steward, Woody, held the week's fresh linens over his arm. "Thought room empty. I come back."

"That's okay, Woody. Get your work done."

"Okay." He quickly stripped the bed and folded it back into the day couch. "Much work today, yes?"

"Why's that?"

"Offload. Eleven hundred hours. Must get cabins done and get down to deck station."

"We're off-loading?"

"Yes. Tanker comes alongside at eleven thirty hours for lightering. Crew at stations eleven hundred hours sharp." He gave a couple swipes at the toilet bowl with a brush, then hung the towels. "Very busy today."

"How's old Charley doing? I haven't seen him in a couple days."

The steward paused as he emptied the wastebasket, a frown pulling his black eyebrows together. "Still a little sick. He works okay, but much coughing. Coughs up some blood. Maybe leaves ship at Cape Town."

"Won't he lose his job if he does that?"

An unhappy shrug. It wasn't something Woody wanted to consider.

"Do you help off-load?"

"Yes. Everybody must work then."

"Same ship every time?"

"Oh, yes." An angry, rising screech of rapid Chinese floated up the stairway. Woody snapped back to his work. "Must go, Mr. Raifah. Very busy now. Chief Steward is very angry."

Around ten hundred hours, the sun-glinted white of a ship's superstructure, like the tip of a distant iceberg, broke the line of horizon off the starboard bow. Gradually, the white speck drew nearer, swinging in a wide arc to a parallel course as its hull lifted above the curve of the sea. The *Aurora* had slowed, taking miles to coast to a speed that scarcely created a bow wave. Each throb of its giant screw was a distinct shudder that trembled the ship like a slow heartbeat. Cautiously, gingerly, the two vessels neared each other as the *Aurora*'s crew rigged heavy, thick fenders alongside. Raiford, his small digital camera busy, leaned on the rail of the covered promenade at the side of the main deck. Four brightly colored signal flags blossomed from the mast of the other ship and fluttered for twenty or thirty seconds before being replaced by another string. Raiford could not read the flags, but he read their implication: neither vessel was using radio communication because they did not want to take the chance of being overheard.

A moment later the signal flags bobbed out of sight, jerked down the mast by unseen hands. A semaphore light winked pairs of dots followed by a message. It was straight Morse code and Raiford had no trouble deciphering that: "Verify three knots 185S." After a pause, the shorthand blink for "Roger, message received" followed by another shorthand signal that Raiford could not decipher.

It probably meant Continue Course or Exercise Maneuver. Within minutes the smaller ship began to drift closer, its hull's rust-streaked red paint standing so high out of the water that the black paint above it was barely washed by the heave of the blue seas. Thickly woven mats protected its flank against any impact with the *Aurora,* and a fast stream of water showed that she was still pumping ballast and rising even higher in preparation for on-loading. If he had a printout of the transfer plan, Raiford could have said exactly how much water was coming out of which compartment, because he had computed the smaller ship's loading program yesterday.

It was a delicate and dangerous maneuver for both vessels. It wasn't just the wakes or the wind that could swing the smaller ship against the low-riding *Aurora Victorious*. Like all VLCCs, the *Aurora* was so large that smaller ships which carelessly ventured too close could be drawn into a collision by its magnetic field. Raiford appreciated the time-consuming care with which the captains inched their vessels closer and closer.

Now he could make out faces scattered along the ship's rail and staring back across the narrowing sea churning with the two ships' bow waves. As Raiford took more photographs, he heard the bridge door open behind him and looked over his shoulder to see Third Officer Li.

The man, surprised to find Raiford, glanced over his own shoulder down the passageway. But the work parties had already mustered and the bridge deck was empty.

"Thought you'd be asleep, Li. Not your watch, is it?"

"No. But I never see this done before. Very interesting."

"This isn't usually done?"

"Oh, no—not at sea. Usually it's done in safe water. Calm water. Tie up to a mooring and off-load to a lighter ship using very long hoses, like in the Virgin Islands." He shook his head, intent on the closing vessel. "Doing it under way is very difficult, very dangerous. Must keep headway to steer both ships, but much—" He held his hands out palms down and waggled them from side to side. "Makes steering very difficult even for the automatic pilot. And one rub"—his hands whisked together—"boom!"

"You've never seen this done before," Raiford asked again.

"No. But it saves time, the captain says. Time is money, yes?"

"Confucius said that too?"

He laughed. "No. Mr. Pressler." The laugh went away. "You have a big fight with him, yes?"

"I guess that's no secret."

"No. Not much secret on a ship." He stood beside Raiford, head not quite as high as the big man's shoulder. "Pressler is a very angry man inside. Captain Boggs is . . . weak. He's not strong like a captain should be. Listens all the time to Pressler, does what Pressler says." A shake of his head. "This is not a happy ship."

They both agreed on that. "What do you know about this other tanker, Li? Where does it take the oil it loads?"

"Maybe Rangoon. Maybe Singapore. Maybe that's why we sail way out to the middle of the Indian Ocean. Makes eighteen, maybe twenty hours longer to Cape Town for us—very expensive for us. So the offload to this other ship must make a lot of money."

Raiford nodded: twenty million or more. On a maneuver far out of the main shipping lanes, using radio silence. Eighteen or twenty hours' sailing time lost—just about the same amount of time needed to shut down at sea and tighten the steam fittings, according to Henderson. If Raiford was writing a mystery novel, he'd say the plot was getting thicker. "How much do you get paid, Li?"

"Two hundred fifty dollars a month. Plus bunk and mess. Good pay." A slightly less happy smile. "Well, pretty good.

Not so good as you English or Americans, but it's okay for now. Pretty soon I can work up to second officer. Someday captain. Then I make good money!"

Somewhere on the foredeck the Tannoy bleated for the work parties to stand to their transfer stations. Raiford leaned out to photograph along the ship's rail. A half-dozen sailors far down the green deck clustered around the stubby boom at the loading manifold. Another two or three sprinted toward them on ship's bicycles. The semaphore on the smaller ship flashed again, but Raiford caught only the latter part of the message, "for loading." He glanced at his watch—11:08. Eight minutes behind schedule and that cost the *Aurora*'s owners another thirty or so dollars. He murmured into the small camera's microphone "Tankers connected, oil transferring."

Then he asked Li, "What would happen if someone moved the Plimsoll mark up on that tanker over there?"

"The Plimsoll?" Li, eyebrows lifted, stared at the ship. "Be very dangerous! The safety margin's gone and ship can swamp very easy. Maybe even break apart in rough water. Too much stress on the hull, yes? Would want damn good insurance on the hull, yes?" He squinted. "The Plimsoll looks okay."

"Would you sail on a ship with a false Plimsoll?"

"Oh, no! No way, José! Raise the Plimsoll, and the ship swamps. Lower the Plimsoll, and the ship rolls bottom up. No—too much danger!"

Raiford decided Li would sleep better not knowing about the *Aurora*'s false Plimsoll. On the deck below, the crew became active. The roll and pitch of the lighter vessel made transferring the hoses an intricate maneuver. Struggling in the sea's turbulent heaving and the *Aurora*'s massive but almost submerged bow wave, the smaller vessel tossed and bobbed while one of its crewmen tried again and again to throw a line across the ocean foaming and hissing between the ships.

The black dot of a weighted monkey's fist sailed out, fell short, and skipped crazily across the ridges of boiling foam as it was repeatedly hauled back. Finally a sailor on deck leaned far out to snag the pilot line with a boat hook, like, Raiford thought, Rossi might have attempted. It was quickly drawn tight to lead the heavier cable attached to it. Then a pulley was attached to the heavier cable and used to lift a hose from the empty vessel to the *Aurora*'s manifold.

This close, his camera's telephoto could pick out details of the ship as Raiford loaded the camera's memory chip. Her name, under a coat of rust and grime, showed that even oil pirates had a touch of wit—the *Stormy Petrol*. From her taffrail flew a flag of three broad horizontal bands—red, yellow, green—with some kind of design in the center: a lion or a palm tree. Like the *Aurora*, that vessel's island was at the stern and its hull stretched toward its bow. Unlike the *Aurora*, the *Stormy Petrol* had several pairs of cargo masts—forward, center, and just in front of the island. A row of six cargo hatches had covers mounted on tracks to open laterally. The pipes that moved liquid cargo were placed at the sides along the ship's rails. A single stack above the bridge slanted back.

The offload went through the lunch hour without a break for chow. A figure—it looked like Pressler—continuously ran a long measuring stick in and out of various inspection plates to monitor oil levels. It was early afternoon before the *Stormy Petrol*'s Klaxon gave a brassy howl that was answered by the deeper, hoarse steam of the *Aurora*'s whistle. The hoses and lines were dropped from the *Aurora Victorious* into the churning sea, and, even while they were being hauled aboard, the *Stormy Petrol* veered sharply to starboard away from danger. The signal light on the wing of its navigation bridge flickered a brief message and its wake deepened in a sharp arc toward the eastern horizon. Raiford felt the *Aurora*'s engines throb harder and faster.

As the *Stormy Petrol* became smaller and smaller, he sensed relief among the crew and realized that his own shoulders, tight with anxiety while the two vessels had run so dangerously close, were now drooping with weary relaxation. The complete transfer maneuver had taken almost five hours, not counting the hours to slow the *Aurora*. It was time enough to deliver the *Aurora*'s foul-weather jettison plus the illegal overage. Far down the deck, a work party secured the fenders that had been placed over the side as feeble protection against a collision and explosion. Another group, nagged by the Tannoy, had begun to hose spilled oil from the deck. The loudspeaker bleated again, this time singling out Raiford: "Electronics officer to the loading control room—electronics officer to the loading control room."

XXII

Julie explained to Mack what Audrey Bennett had discovered about the captain of the *Aurora Victorious*.

"Where the hell did he get all that money? What's going on, Julie?"

"He's not the only one." Beyond the glass door of the small sundries shop, the traffic of Great Russell Street hissed and rumbled.

"What do you mean?"

"Audrey also found out that the first mate, Gerald Pressler, recently sold his house in Folkston. He took quite a loss on it because it's near the Chunnel—all the residential property values dropped after the Chunnel went in. But he bought another place in Kent, outside Canterbury near Petham, worth twice as much. And he paid cash."

The other end of the line was silent. The public telephone, more secure than a cell phone, was in an alcove just beyond this shop's small post office. Rows of newspapers filled a rack along the opposite wall. The other shelves held magazines, candy, tobacco, medical nostrums, toilet articles, and a variety of things people tended to carry in pocket or purse.

Finally he asked, "Anybody else become a big spender?"

"Funny you should ask. Marine Carriers's agent who sold the policy on the *Golden Dawn*, Mrs. Fleenor, paid off her daughter's medical bills three months ago. Seventeen thousand dollars. Know anything about that, Stan?"

"Dorothy? Aw, no—"

"That's a lot of money."

"Where'd you get that information?"

"It came up on her credit history." Julie added, "She bought a new car, too. Again: cash."

"Aw, man, not Dorothy! Man, I should've caught that, but I never . . ."

Julie let her silence agree: Mack was right—he should have caught that.

"All right . . . I'll check out her finances in detail."

"But wait"—her voice echoed a television pitch—"there's more. The widow of the captain of the *Golden Dawn*, Olivia Minkey, recently sold her house and moved to Rio. I'm trying to get a report on her lifestyle there."

He considered that. "The *Aurora* and the *Golden Dawn* again. There has to be some kind of connection."

"Right. I wish Bert had made more notes." Not that the detective had expected to be killed. But Julie would have to reexamine all Herberling's papers, even the handwriting and stray pen marks for hints at any thoughts that lay behind the words on the page.

"Julie, if all these people are making that much money, we're talking a lot of money to be made. But I haven't heard anyone scream about losing that much. It's got to come from somewhere—I mean, it just doesn't grow on trees. A bite that big has to be hurting someone."

"Three possibilities: One, the bitee can't make waves because it's illegal money. Two, the bitee's under threat of some kind if he does complain. Three, the bitee doesn't know he's been bitten."

"You lean toward any of those?"

"Not yet. I want to go over Herberling's file again. And I'm hoping my dad has come up with something."

"Get through to him again?"

"No." She added, "Nothing from, and they're not answering calls."

"That's worrisome."

It was. More than Mack knew. "Especially since someone laid a hit on me." She told him about the excitement at Hampstead.

"Did he hurt you?"

"Nothing to speak of."

"Jesus. Well, I guess that means you're on the right track."

"So was Herberling."

"Yeah. Poor bastard. Do you want support, Julie? I have contacts there who owe me a couple of favors."

"No. I can handle myself."

The telephone was quiet a moment. "Okay—you're in the business, you know what you're risking. But keep looking over your shoulder, Julie."

She intended to. "I'm building up some hefty costs for information, Stan. Both here and in Rio. It's more than my clients need, and more than I should bill them for. Can Marine Carriers Worldwide help? Even if we don't find anything against Hercules?"

"I'll talk to them—it's becoming their case, too. I'll see if they'll throw in something." His promise was conditional, but not his next comment. "But if we do save Marine Carriers Worldwide money, there'll be plenty to cover those expenses."

After she hung up, Julie stared at the cover of a magazine whose bare-breasted and whitely smiling model stared back for an equally long time. Then she put her BT card in the slot and dialed the office in Denver. If she were aboard the *Aurora Victorious*, she would be trying every conceivable avenue of communication. And she and her father often thought along the same lines.

XXIII

Shockley gave Raiford new off-loading figures to replace those currently in the Lodicator.

"This is what we're taking to the Caribbean now?" Raiford scanned down the printout that had arrived from London.

The second mate nodded.

"Won't Pierce have time to install these figures after he gets back? We're what, thirty, forty days out of the Virgin Islands?"

"First Mate wants the figures run now. Says do them before you leave ship. That's all I know."

"Pierce's helicopter is the one that will take me to Cape Town, right?"

"Right. Two days from now." Shockley cleared his throat. "Usually comes in midmorning, so you'll want to be packed up early."

"Can't say I'll be all that sorry to leave the old *Aurora*. But it has been a real learning experience."

"Just make certain you're packed and ready to go on time. And take everything—company policy is not to forward personal effects left aboard."

"Right. Even my shadow."

"Even that." Shockley paused as if he were going to add something. Instead, he stared for a long moment at Raiford. The intent, worried look in his eyes gave way to some kind of blankness as if he willed something to be erased from his mind. Then he ducked through the loading control room doorway and closed it firmly behind him.

The mood at the evening meal was a lot lighter than it had been at breakfast. Even Raiford was included in general remarks that passed up and down the table. The cause, he noted, was Pressler. Though the first mate still ignored Raiford, he was in good spirits and laughed at something the dour chief engineer had muttered over his soup. The laugh wasn't an attractive sight, and there was a note of malice in the sound. But it was a welcome change from the icy silence of the preceding days, and Raiford guessed that the first mate's good spirits had been generated either by the thought of the supernumerary's coming departure or by adding up the man's share of the day's stolen oil.

"That was quite a maneuver today." Raiford passed the bread across to Henderson. "Off-loading while we're under way."

The junior engineering officer nodded and swallowed to clear his mouth. "Never lightered that way aboard any other vessel. Must save the owners a pile of money, though. No time lost tying up, no berthing or pilots' fees. Be a bit of a gamble in any heavier seas, though."

"Has the *Aurora* ever off-loaded like that in bad weather?"

"Not since I've been aboard, thank God. Wouldn't want to, either. I don't care how much money it saves the owners. All it takes to set off an empty tanker is one tiny spark, and running that close alongside . . ." He shook his head. "Bad enough living on one of these floating bombs without banging two of them together."

At the head of the table, Pressler, still smiling, caught the last words. "Just remember, young Mr. Henderson, you could well owe your job to today's little maneuver. Saving money for the owners might allow them to keep this old vessel in service for another couple of years. Wouldn't you agree, Mr. Shockley, that the money's worth the risk?"

"Eh?" The second mate's pudgy cheeks turned pink. "Oh—yes. Of course."

"Of course!" The fresh scar on Pressler's lip whitened with the stretch of his grin. "So you see, young Mr. Henderson, regardless of the weather—fair or foul—it pays us all to take a chance now and then. If the owners feel it's worth it, that is."

"Yes, sir. I just meant I wouldn't like to off-load under way in foul weather. I mean, it really could be a dangerous maneuver in heavy seas." He cleared his throat nervously and looked around the table for support. "Empty tanker alongside and all. Couldn't it?"

Pressler was still playing with the young officer. "Seafaring's a dangerous business in weather good or bad, Mr. Henderson. We take our pay and we take our risks. You can vouch for that, can't you, Mr. Bowman?"

The chief engineer's close-cropped gray hair tilted toward the table as he sopped up the remainder of his gravy with a piece of bread. "Don't like to tell you your business, Pressler. But it's getting on six bells."

"So it is—so it is. All right, people, let's finish up so the steward can clear the mess."

Anxious as ever to have the meal over, the steward hovered in the galley doorway. But despite his words, Pressler was in no hurry to finish his custard. The other officers were bound by custom to stay until the first mate rose to lead the parade into the wardroom for coffee.

"You'll be leaving us day after tomorrow, Mr. Raiford."

"All good things must end, Mr. Pressler."

The first mate, elbows braced on the table, folded his thick hands beneath his chin and nodded. Smiled. "Indeed so— indeed so."

Raiford smiled in return. "But I've enjoyed the voyage—a real holiday cruise."

The mate's good nature hardened into something else as his knuckles made a muffled crunch. But he kept smiling. "I'm pleased to hear that. And I hope no misunderstandings have clouded our acquaintance."

"No misunderstandings at all."

"Pleased, indeed." He shoved his chair back. "Well, time to let the steward do his work, eh?"

This time, Raiford took his coffee in the wardroom instead of his quarters. Shockley, by himself at a corner of the bar, nursed a pint of bitters. He looked surprised and uncomfortable as Raiford settled on a stool beside him.

"First Mate seems jolly tonight."

"Yes—ah—the offloading. . . . Yes."

"Any last wishes by way of electronics?"

His pale eyes blinked as Raiford's words registered. "Last wishes? No—ah, I don't think so. I'll let you know in the morning. Be certain you pack up early—everything." He dipped his face to his beer.

"I'll be ready. See you at breakfast." Raiford heaved off the barstool.

Mouth full, the second officer nodded.

The silence of Raiford's quarters, emphasized by the steady wheeze of the ventilation system, allowed his mind to run free, and the coldest thought was that when Rossi went overboard, the *Aurora* could not waste time lowering a boat to pick him up. It would have taken time to unhook the hoses from the *Stormy Petrol*, miles to bring a ship the size of the *Aurora* to a halt, time to lower a boat and send it back, and more time to look for a single man in a wide ocean. Then bring both ships alongside once more, reconnect the hoses, and complete the offload. Ten, maybe twelve hours for the entire maneuver— another half day's sailing to cover up. Rossi simply had not been worth it, so they left him. Then they'd had to hide both the manner as well as the place of his death because the *Aurora* was not supposed to be doing what she was where she was.

So they made up the story of his fall down a ladder and his burial at sea.

A soft tapping broke into his thoughts. He opened the door to find Woody, eyes wide with anxiety. "Mr. Raifah, sah—Sam asks please you meet him tonight on fantail at two bells. Very important, please, sah. You meet him there, yes?"

"Two bells?"

"Very important, yes?"

"Sure, Woody."

"Thank you, sah. Must go now." The man almost sprinted down the carpeted hall toward the stairs as if Raiford might chase after him.

The sea wind was cold. No window showed light in the aft side of the bridge that towered above Raiford. At one in the morning, the only people awake were the navigation crew who would be on the bridge staring forward over the blackened foredeck. At the tip of the radar mast above the bridge, the middle running light made one of the brighter stars. Beneath Raiford's rubber soles, the steel plating quivered with the straining effort of the engines running near top speed. They were cruising two, maybe three knots faster than they had before, small hourly gains that—over days and nights of steady cruising—could add up to the one or two hundred miles the *Aurora* had swung off-course. If they were lucky, as Li had once mentioned, the retail price of oil might fall too low in the States and the *Aurora* would receive orders for slow steaming. Tankers in route provided oil companies convenient and relatively inexpensive storage for crude until America's refineries began to run short again and the price of gas or heating oil could be shoved back up a nickel or dime a gallon. It was a price manipulation conveniently outside the American jurisdiction and unchallenged by the large number of American politicians whose cozy ties to the oil industry gave them blind appreciation for its large donations to their reelection funds.

Raiford glanced at the dim green pips on his watch. Twenty after the hour and still no Sam. Stiff from the cold, Raiford moved out of the shadow of the boat davit toward the warmth of the nearest promenade. But before he reached it, something moved quickly along the rail toward him. Raiford ducked to meet the charging figure and felt the heavy, stunning blow of a club glance down the side of his head and deep into his shoulder. Through the flash of hot pain and flaring circles of red and yellow, he struck back with a reflexive jab. His fist banged solidly against flesh to knock away the attacking shape long enough for Raiford to clear his vision. A raised arm came toward him again and, pivoting, Raiford struck out with a sidekick that thudded all the way up to his hip. A whiny, grunting sound came from the shadow as it fell away, but running feet from the other side of the ship replaced it. Raiford snapped a frontkick that caught the middle of the new shadow and flung it, arms wide, to clatter heavily against the deck. But the first shadow was up and coming again, its club or iron bar humming savagely through the air.

Raiford caught a numbing blow on the back of his forearm and drove his other arm in a stiff-fingered, upward jab as deep as the assailant's lungs. He yanked his hand out of the soft flesh, hoping the shock would rupture the man's organs. A steamy breath spewed the odor of garlic as the club swung feebly at Raiford. He pivoted and cracked a sidekick at the nearest dimly seen leg, his heel jarring into bone and driving the shape down beside the scupper that echoed with the sound of the roiled sea hissing below.

The second man was on his feet with some kind of guttural noise. Raiford drove an elbow into his dim face before they grappled. Three shapes tangled with grunts and the smack of fists. Two figures broke away and the third, staggering back, dived in again, going low for the legs. The almost silent clump of struggling shadows jolted and reeled against the wire cable of the ship's open rail, and two shapes froze together in a sudden balance of locked arms. The third figure jumped hard at them, and arms and hunched shoulders broke loose again in a blur of movement that swung one of the shapes high over the rail. It hung, momentarily silhouetted against the night sky. Then it plunged wordlessly out of sight into the hissing turmoil of foam that sucked and bubbled along the hull.

Motionless, the two remaining figures stared down and back at the disappearing wake. Then one turned and sprinted for the nearest door, the other close behind.

XXIV

Julie pressed in the code to play the office recorder. Maybe something had come in from her dad during the last few hours. Maybe he had called that number instead of her mobile phone. The mechanical voice in Denver said there were three messages and she tapped the pen on the paper pad, waiting for the slow announcements of day and hour and length of message. But the only results were a reminder of the next meeting of the Professional Private Investigators Association, an inquiry about rates for uncovering an ex-spouse's assets, and a recorded sales pitch trying to talk the office recorder into a free trip to Las Vegas.

She stared through the large window at Russell Square and its trees slowly turning black with night. In Denver, autumn would be coming down from the mountains as cold rain. It wouldn't be long before it turned to snow. Here, dusk was made deeper by the glare of headlights in the streets and, among the square's trees, the soft glow of lamps.

Plugging in her laptop, she switched it on and typed the Internet access code and office security number. Opening the mailbox she read the dark print of new messages. Then, scarcely breathing, she printed a hard copy. While the printer hummed, she quickly placed a call to Mack.

XXV

Raiford had chased his man down the ringing steel ladders into the bowels of the ship. But the cramped space of the engine room, its tight corners and snagging pipes, valves, and handles worked against the larger man. The other—smaller, quicker—knew the ship better than Raiford, knew shortcuts through narrow gaps, knew the hatches that led from one compartment to another, knew the quickest way to ferret his way into shadows and hollows made even darker by the leaking steam.

Finally, gasping, soaked with sweat and steam, Raiford gave up. His prey, desperate to keep Raiford's broad hands off his neck, had flitted into shadows at a juncture of catwalks, and Raiford had no idea which way the man went. It wasn't Alfred. Raiford had seen that man's face wide-eyed with sudden fear as he struggled voicelessly to reach across space while he plunged down the ship's side into the boiling ocean.

Raiford climbed the ladders with a weariness that was not of flesh alone. Alfred might be going under for the last time about now. Unless he had been sucked into the ship's screw when he hit the water. That would be better, Raiford told himself. Get it over fast. Maybe mercifully numb from the shock of the fall. Or, better, unconscious. It would be worse to fight back to the surface only to watch the ship's red and green running lights disappear over the narrow horizon, and then to grow aware of the awful isolation of an empty sea at night. To know that this far outside the shipping lanes you would not be saved. To know that the ship would not slow for you. That no matter how hard you struggled to stay afloat, nor how long you managed, it would not be enough. No matter how many times you searched the black sea and pitiless stars for help, you would sink from this living world surrounded by an isolation as awful as death itself.

He stood beside an open door on the Level One deck and stared down the luminous wake to where the man might be still struggling. Just as Rossi had struggled. It could have been Raiford instead of Alfred. Was supposed to be. Raiford had seen enough decent people slain by the hands of the indecent that the loss of Alfred shouldn't bother him. What he should feel was satisfaction that the bastard who tried to kill him received what he intended to give. But there was no satisfaction. Not even a feeling of relief at having escaped. Just a black weariness at the thought of having flung the man into the sea.

Maybe because of the way the man could be dying this very second. Maybe Alfred, alone, growing cold and numb, floated on his back and stared at a sky whose blackness would soon thin in the east. Soon Alfred might see the red and yellow streaks of an empty and final dawn. Maybe he was hanging on for that: to die in the light instead of in the dark.

The ship's bell chimed faintly: four strokes of the second watch. The galley crew would begin to turn out and the day's routine would start. They would include Woody who, like all stewards, stood galley duty before turning to the officers' quarters and then moving on to the ship's work. A twelve-, sometimes fourteen-hour day, and—when the ship's operations demanded—a twenty-four-hour day. All for bed, beans, and thirty a month. A man working that hard for that little could be tempted, and Raiford wondered how much Alfred or even Pressler might have paid the steward to lure him into the trap.

Through the portholes of the galley came the clattering sounds of metal pans and glassware. A few men wearing cotton drawers and thong shower sandals, towels and soap in their hands, straggled into and out of the common bathroom. Raiford nodded to one sleepy face that squinted up at him with sleepy surprise.

"Woody's cabin? You know Woody?"

"Ah—" He pointed down the walkway behind him and held up three fingers.

"Three doors down?"

A nod.

He passed the open entry to the crew's bath and toilets with its sounds of running water and occasional echoing Chinese. At the door, he knocked.

Motionless drapes sealed the cabin window. It took four tries, each louder than the last, before the latch rattled and the door opened a crack to show Woody's face. The man's eyes bulged as he gazed up at Raiford.

"Good to see you, too, Woody. I can't tell you how good it is."

"Mr. Raifah—" He stood like a man staring at a dangerous and threatening animal.

Raiford pushed into the room. The small cubicle was filled with a single bunk mounted above a bureau, a tiny metal sink in one corner, a leaf table and chair on the facing wall. "Why, Woody? Who told you to?"

"Mr. Raifah—"

"I heard you the first time." He placed the chair in front of the closed door and settled into it, smiling at the slender man who stood flatfooted in his baggy drawers. "Why did you send me to the fantail?"

"Mr.—"

"Yeah, I know. Mr. Raifah. Why, Woody? Who told you to send me there?"

"Chief Steward tells me, sah! Mr. Johnny. He says tell Mr. Raifah to meet Sam on the fantail at two bells of first watch." The man's bony chest rose and fell with a deep sigh. "Very glad to see you, Mr. Raifah—very happy!" He wagged his head. "Very much afraid."

"Alfred and somebody else tried to kill me, Woody. Do you know who it was? The man with Alfred?"

The wag turned into emphatic shaking. "No! Chief Steward only tells me to tell you. That's all! Nothing about Alfred— nothing about trying to . . . to kill you, sah!"

"You didn't know they would try to kill me?"

"No, sah! No, no!"

"But you were afraid."

Another deep sigh that made his ribs rise like fingers beneath the taut skin. "Yes, sah. Maybe hurt you, sah. First Mate is your enemy, sah. You're a good man—you saved Charley, you helped Sam. But Chief Steward is boss. . . . Is officers' business, not mine. Chief Steward is boss."

"Who helps Alfred, Woody? Who does Alfred hang around with?"

"Maybe Yun Hyon—Korean man who works the donkey engine. Maybe Sung Ching. Shandong Province. Sung Ching's not from Taiwan. You find Alfred, yes? Make him tell you."

"Alfred's dead. Went over the side."

"Ai."

"And now you're going to run and tell the chief steward that I'm alive and you know where I am, is that right?"

The man's black eyes showed they understood Raiford's words and what they implied. His mouth, protuberant with crooked and tobacco-stained teeth, tightened. "No!" His narrow shoulders grew wider. "Not tell Chief Steward. Not tell nobody. It's officers' business, not mine!" The black eyes grew wet. "You're a good man, sah. Not go tell on you!"

"It may be officers' business, Woody, but I need help." Raiford studied the clenched face. "I need the camera that's in my bureau drawer and I need a place to hide until the helicopter comes. Pressler's looking for me right now. He'll have a pistol and he'll sure as hell use it."

The man nodded. "It's true."

"The camera and a place to hide. You understand?"

"I understand. You stay here—my cabin. I'll go get the camera." He began pulling on his coveralls. "You're safe here."

Raiford shook his head. "Pressler will search every cabin. Where else?"

A blink of eyes as he thought. "The fan room. Many machineries to hide behind. Easy to see Mr. Pressler come."

The steward led him half running down the companionway to a ladder. They dropped belowdecks and Woody headed aft toward a crowded section of the ship that Raiford had not seen before. Opening a small hatch, Woody went down ill-lit ladders into the tighter confines of the converging plates of the ship's stern. There he opened an even smaller hatch.

Sweating, his breath growing shallow as they descended, Raiford could feel the steel close around him as their heels thudded down the metal stairs from one dimly lit grate to the next. Down and down again, and still farther down into the steam that filled the noisy and cramped belly of the ship.

The glow of Raiford's watch told him it was almost noon when he heard the squeal of a watertight door being opened. The beam of a flashlight swung through the thin steam and dim light of the few bulbs serving the compartment. The fuzzy circle played along the tangle of steel shapes as Raiford tucked himself into the darker shadow of a ship's strut. Then the light swung away as the searcher climbed back up and the rusty hinges squealed shut. Then a long time passed—long enough that he lost track of day or night and only Woody's hasty visits with smuggled food oriented him to time. He slept and waked, dozed again, dropping off into sounder sleep and waked at something—a minor shift in the rpm of the giant propeller shaft that whirred and hummed not two arms' length away in the steam.

When Woody brought the next meal, lunch, he spoke quickly. "They still look for you, Mr. Raifah." His voice scarcely carried over the deep reverberation of the spinning shaft in its massive sealed bearings. "But you're okay here."

"Yeah." Raiford wasn't. The damp bulkheads had crept in on him until it felt as if he either had to break through the stifling walls or run screaming toward the light and openness of the main deck. But he didn't. He willed his mind away from the contracting walls. Sweating in the steam, he reviewed his camera's digital photographs of the *Stormy Petrol,* forced himself to study the *Aurora's* wires and conduits that coursed around the grimy bulkheads and overhead, sought patterns in the patches of rust and mold that disfigured plates and beams. And tried to stay alert, even in sleep, for any sound of feet coming down a ladder.

The next meal—supper—came in another cardboard box, this one labeled Winslow's Frozen Meat. "Cook ask me where I go. I tell him the engineering officer wants food—is working on a boiler and can't come to the saloon. Wants food brought. Cook says okay, but he maybe finds out different soon."

"The helicopter's due this afternoon, right?"

Woody shrugged. "Nobody says. Must quick go now, Mr. Raifah. I'll come back at noontime."

Squatting against the ship's trembling skin, Raiford's shoes pushed up a ridge of rust and oily grime from the steel deck. The fan room was never cleaned; there were too many other jobs for the small crew, and this corner of the vessel was left to its decades-old rust and its cockroaches.

By now, Raiford had a half-dozen boxes mashed flat and hidden far under the grated metal housing that covered one of the loudly whirring ventilation fans. Shiny, dark spots fed on the oil and scraps that clung to the cardboard. As he watched the cluster of cockroaches, the distant squeak of an opening hatch cut through the throbbing noise to catch his ear. This time, the flashlight beam did not stop on the landing above but moved steadily down, closer, the shadowy figure behind the glare cautious and pausing to probe the cone of light into the steam. Raiford pulled deeper into the recess between a beam and the curve of hull.

The light kept coming. At the foot of the ladder it searched carefully into angles and shadows. Raiford's only chance was to crawl beneath the glistening, humming shaft of the propeller, to move across the narrow angle of the ship's stern into the dimness of the other side. It would be a tight fit. The steel shaft spun like a roller to snag his clothes and twist his body into a broken pulp.

But the flashlight came closer.

He lay on his back in the greasy dirt and rust and sucked his chest and belly as flat as he could. Pressing under the spinning steel, he felt its warmth and wind against his ear and cheek, felt the top of his head push against the wriggling life drawn by the food-tainted boxes. Inch at a time, forcing out his breath, he pulled with his elbows and shoved with his heels through the grit. Grime dredged into his collar and waist, and he felt spiky, prickly legs begin to feel their way hungrily past his ear and down his neck.

Over the bulge that was his knee, he saw the flashlight probe the corner where he had slept, and he wriggled faster. Hot, oily water dripped from the shaft that whirled just beyond his nose. The beam swung into the starboard recess and played along the bright gleam of the spinning steel. Yanking himself from under the shaft, Raiford lifted himself high off the deck by bracing his arms between a fan housing and the bulkhead. A spray of light swept under the shaft and across the grime of his passage to show the rusty weld of the port side of the ship below his braced and trembling legs. Hanging in the dimness, he watched it quickly swing left and right, then pull back. The gleam moved away. Gingerly, quietly, arms and legs quivering from effort, he lowered himself to the deck and waited, fingers gouging for the scurrying, horny feet that scratched at his chest and armpits.

The flashlight swung along the haze-dimmed catwalk to

the port ladder and up and out of sight. A faintly clanging squeal of rusty metal told him that the access door in the bulkhead had been dogged down again. His watch said three forty-five.

Woody waited nervously for the plate and silverware while Raiford ate. He gulped the cold eggs and porridge and washed it down with coffee that, mercifully, was still hot in its Thermos pitcher. He left little for the roaches—let them work for their food like everyone else. "It's four bells of the third watch, right? Nine in the morning?"

"Yes, sah—sorry I come so late—cook keeps his eye on me and I have to come when I can."

"No problem, Woody. You're doing fine. What's happening topside?"

"Crew's very worried. Cannot find you. Cannot find Alfred. Officers alla time go around with wrinkled faces. Crew's very afraid you die. Think maybe you and Alfred go over the side together. I want to tell them but I do not."

"Good. Keep it quiet. I have to get up there, Woody. When the helicopter brings Mr. Pierce, I want to make a run for it. Can you get me up to the main deck without being seen?"

The Chinese man thought for a long moment, then smiled. "You come to my quarters, wait there, yes? Then you go on deck through the stack housing when the chopper comes."

"What if they search the crew's quarters?"

"Already do it. My room, everybody's. They look in, come in and look around, say it's inspection for cleanliness." He snorted. "Cleanliness! Mr. Pressler, he wears gun and makes inspection hisself. But it's okay now. You come." He glanced down Raiford's filthy and oil-stained clothes. "I'll bring clean clothes from your cabin. You take a shower in the crew's head—no one's there now, yes?"

"A shower? Oh, man, let's do it!"

XXVI

The earliest flight Stanley Mack could get—a 5:15 A.M. from Kennedy—landed at Gatwick in midafternoon. Julie glimpsed the man fidgeting in the line among other aliens who waited to get their passports stamped for entry. Finally, a customs agent processed Mack's passport and he hurried toward her, talking even before they shook hands. "I made some calls from the airplane to Marine Carriers. Told Mr. Mohler a little about it. He notified the London office that we're on our way. They're sending a car to pick us up and Mohler said the London office will stay open until we get there." He glanced up at the electric message board, but neither his nor Julie's name flashed across it. "Let me get some money changed."

Another queue, this one shorter and faster, then out to the covered sidewalk that fronted a busy pick-up zone. At the far end and weaving among clusters of newly arrived travelers and their luggage, a liveried driver held up a hand-lettered card that said "Marine Carriers." He chanted anxiously, "Mr. Mack? Mr. Stanley Mack, please? Mr. Mack?"

"Here!"

Julie and Mack chased after the booted legs and piled into the limousine's backseat as the driver hastily thudded Mack's scarred suitcase into the boot. When the vehicle cleared the access roads and began to pick up speed on the express highway north, Stan sagged wearily against the seat. "Christ, I didn't think I'd make it. I've been running since I got your call last night. This morning, I mean." The gray-faced man fumbled in the small refrigerator for a bottle of lime-flavored soda water. "I'm getting too old for this." He drank deeply and sighed again, tired eyes watching but not seeing the soggy black trees glide swiftly past. "All right, let me tell you what I've found out. First, there's no such vessel registered with any nation—flag of convenience or otherwise. No such vessel listed in the ship directories. None covered by any of the maritime insurers. The *Stormy Petrol* seems to be a pirate ship."

Mack's information filled in one of the suspicions given birth by the e-mail Julie had received. And she provided additional information uncovered by Audrey Bennett: "Olivia Minkey—she's the widow of the captain of the *Golden Dawn*—bought a very nice finca in Rio. For cash. She also paid cash for her new furnishings, hired a household staff, stocked up supplies, bought a new Mercedes, new clothes. All cash."

"More than her husband's life insurance can account for?" asked Mack.

Julie smiled. "His policy, taken out six weeks before the *Golden Dawn* was lost, paid one hundred fifty thousand pounds. Audrey's contact in Rio estimates her expenses so far at around three hundred thousand dollars. That doesn't leave her much to live on unless she has a lot of other income." Julie added, "But then she also has a new bank account in the Bahamas. Couldn't get access to that, though. And the household staff say she's expecting her husband to join her in Rio in a few weeks."

"Her husband? But . . ." The weariness disappeared and Mack's eyes looked alert. "That's our pirate ship—the *Golden Dawn*!"

Julie nodded. "The widow is not a widow. Her husband's now the pirate captain of the *Stormy Petrol*."

Mack closed his eyes and sighed deeply. "It fits, by God. It fits!" Then, "Anything new from the *Aurora*?"

"Not yet."

"I've been worried about that." His closed eyes frowned. "Wasn't much else to occupy my mind on the flight and I was too wired to sleep. But maybe there's something we can do from this end. New York promised that London will fully and promptly cooperate. Whatever we need, it's ours."

"What can we do and how fast?"

The bloodshot eyes opened to study Julie's taut expression. "Yeah: what and how soon—that's what I've been worrying about."

XXVII

It was eleven forty-five. Raiford had heard nothing of a helicopter's pending arrival. Peeking through the closed drapes
of Woody's window onto the gallery, he could see only two
portholes of gray sky. The distant horizon that occasionally
rose up into the holes showed that the sea, too, was gray.
The monsoon had died out, the *Aurora* had dropped below
the southern trades and their generally fair seas, and now it
was well into the colder waters near the South African cape.
Overcast and windy, but not—he fervently hoped—enough
to keep the helicopter from making its flight. Because he was
definitely not going back down into that cramped and stifling
roach hotel.

A soft scratching on the door and Raiford cracked it
open to show a very nervous Woody. "You ready now, Mr.

Raifah? Go aft. Charley waits for you at the stack-housing ladder."

The gallery curved with the ship's hull and Raiford strode quickly past the windows of the crew's quarters to the ladder aft. As he neared it, Charley's grinning face popped down from the overhead hatch. "This way—hurry, sah!"

Raiford, camera strap around his wrist, followed the sprinting man across the main deck and through the entry to the stack housing. There, Charley motioned for silence and disappeared up another ladder. Then an arm beckoned and Raiford went up to find a small corridor flanked by locked doors. Metal plates identified the ship's store, two double-locked reefers, and the laundry facility. Charley fitted a key into a door that said POOL MAINTENANCE and fumbled with the lock. It seemed to take a long time, and Raiford was increasingly aware of voices floating up from the main deck, of sounds of life from the bridge forward. Finally the door clicked open.

"Okay, sah! When helicopter comes, you can run forward from here, yes? And I find for you a hiding spot." Charley pointed to the bulge of the swimming pool tank that pressed through the ceiling almost to the floor. "You go under there, okay?"

"I can't fit under there, Charley. I'm too big!"

The man looked up and down Raiford's torso. "Too big, yes." He scratched at his cropped black hair. "Okay—stay here. If somebody comes, then you get a lot smaller real fast, yes? Go under there."

"I guess it could happen."

The room was close and narrow, filled by the belly of the metal pool, and had no portholes. The water pump and filter assembly crowded one corner, and in another a cabinet held plastic buckets of pool chemicals and a few maintenance tools. The only sounds were the whine of the water pump and, beneath that, the ship's forced air system. Deepest of all, the flue going up the neighboring stack gave off a visceral rumble, its hot exhaust used to warm the swimming pool's water. This seldom-used space did not have a Tannoy, so Raiford could not hear the ship's bell, the noon announcements of distance traveled in the last twenty-four hours, or any special duty assignments or pages from the bridge. He did near the metallic scrape of a key in the door and moved quickly behind it as it opened.

"Mr. Raifah—Mr. . . . Aii!" Charley gaped over his shoulder at the big shape poised for attack. "It's me!"

"Has it come?"

"Tannoy says ten minutes. Comes at thirteen twenty. We go now."

Raiford could hear the ship's speaker echo in the passageway, "All hands stand clear the forward deck. Helicopter arriving in five minutes. All hands stand clear the forward deck."

This time Charley led down an internal ladder into the engine decks, then forward through the boiler room and past the ship's generators. At another ladder, Charley went up cautiously. Once more the arm beckoned and Raiford followed to the corridor that ran past the crew's galley on the main deck.

Ears alert, they waited for the sound of the helicopter's popping exhaust. Raiford wasn't certain just what he'd tell the pilot when he sprinted down the long deck and tumbled aboard the chopper. But the pilot should be expecting him. The mail, a case of new movies, and Pierce were coming aboard; going out would be the mail, the old movies, and, Raiford fervently hoped, Pierce's temporary replacement. The catch would be when Pressler began shooting. He would have to wait until the helicopter cleared the ship—a stray bullet, a crash aboard ship, any spark near the oil manifold could set the *Aurora* ablaze. But Raiford had no doubt that Pressler would shoot if he could—the helicopter and all aboard it were far less valuable than the stolen oil, and a helicopter crash at sea was not uncommon. Raiford would have to make the pilot understand that danger, and do it the moment he was aboard.

Still no sound of airborne engines.

"Charley, you go on back to work. You don't have to wait here with me."

"It's okay."

"No, it's not okay. If the first mate sees you with me, you're in big trouble. Go on, now—I can handle it from here."

"Okay—I go. Thank you, Mr. Raifah, yes? Good luck, yes?"

"Thanks, Charley. And keep your head down."

The grinning man disappeared. Raiford listened tensely at the doorway and searched the sky.

Until he heard a shout, "There he is!"

Shockley, standing in the doorway at the other end of the corridor, shouted again to someone aft. "Starboard side, main deck. It's him!"

Raiford, stuffing the camera safely inside his shirt, sprinted for the stairway only to see the startled face of a sailor below him who yelled something in Chinese. An instant later, the chief steward and the Korean, Yun Hyon, ran toward the foot of the stairs. Raiford turned upstairs, his long legs taking three steps at a time. Up past the junior officers' level and still up. How he'd manage to get down when the chopper came, he wasn't sure. But he was damned certain he heard the thud of a dozen feet after him and the savagely happy bellow of Pressler, "Get the barstid! Get him, goddamn your eyes—get him!"

Raiford burst through the double doors of the navigation bridge and into the shocked faces of the radioman, the duty helmsman, and Captain Boggs, who, without a word, lunged at Raiford. Twisting away from the captain's flailing arm, Raiford chopped his hand into the man's neck. The captain grunted and fell to a knee, clutching his throat. The radioman, shaking his head no, backed up with his hands raised in surrender and stumbled over the helmsman who tried to hold the wheel steady even as he cowered against the bridge's console.

Raiford's eye lit on the emergency cabinet mounted on the aft bulkhead and he dug his fingers under the metal lip of its locked door. Straining until his shirt seam crackled across his shoulders, he peeled back its metal door and grabbed the Very pistol and a box of shells and sprinted for the ladder up the mast. He was halfway up to the radar scanner when Pressler, pistol in hand, ran onto the open deck below.

"Raiford, goddamn you!"

The first mate leveled his weapon and it popped twice. The puffs of smoke blew quickly away in the strong wind. Raiford heard one bullet sizzle hotly somewhere near his left ear as he flung himself up the last few rungs and onto the small platform high above the bridge. Swiveling open the flare gun, he clicked it shut and quickly fired a round high into the gray sky. Its trail arced up and up to burst in a bright pink flare that smoked and danced as it drifted back toward the gray and wind-chopped ocean.

"Won't do you any good, Raiford. The helicopter's not coming—there is no helicopter!" Another shot punctuated the mate's triumphant yell. "A trick to smoke you out, you barstid!"

"You hear me, Pressler? You hear me?"

"Say what you want to now, damn your eyes, because you are a dead man. I swear by God almighty you are already dead!"

"If I'm dead, you will be too, Pressler. I'll shoot this flare at the oil manifold. I'll send this bucket up like a firecracker!"

The empty whistle of the wind told Raiford that the man heard his threat.

"I've got nothing to lose, Pressler. I'll take you with me!"

"Goddamn—!" Another shot smacked into the metal of the platform and ricocheted off somewhere with a nasal scream.

"Hold it, Pressler—wait!" Shockley's voice cut through the

wind. Raiford eased to the edge of the platform and peeked over. The second mate leaned out of the doorway to the flying bridge. "Wait, damn it—he'll do it. He'll kill us all!"

"That bloody flare gun won't—"

"It might! For God's sake, Pressler, he could spark the hose connections. It's too big a chance." The voice dropped and Shockley, glancing up at the crow's nest, gestured something. Raiford heard the angry snarl of vague, wind-tossed voices. Then Pressler strode to the weather door of the bridge and out of sight. Shockley, shoulders sagging with the weight of his dangling arms, stared up at Raiford. A moment later, a half-dozen men were herded by a screaming Pressler onto the open bridge.

"Up! Goddamn you—get up that ladder and bring him down now!"

The crewmen hung back. Pressler's wide fist grabbed Yun Hyon's neck and drove him like a rag doll to the ladder rungs. "Up!" Pressler waved the pistol. "If he shows his goddamn face, I'll kill him! Up, damn you!"

A few seconds later, Raiford felt the mast quiver as feet climbed slowly. It was stupid of Pressler. Raiford waited. Three fingers of a hand gingerly grasped the edge of the hatchway. Raiford waited. Then the other hand felt for a grip. Raiford waited. Two, three breaths—even Pressler stopped shouting. Then the mast quivered again as Yun lunged upward through the hole in the floor of the crow's nest and Raiford kicked out. His heel caught the side of the man's head to smack it hard against the steel rim of the hatchway, and then Raiford's heel smashed down on the slipping, straining fingers until they yanked out of sight. Raiford felt snagging tingles as the man plummeted along the mast, and then he heard the thud of flesh hitting steel below.

"Send up another one, Pressler!"

No answer.

Raiford scooted to the platform edge and peered cautiously over. Four sailors were dragging Yun's broken body into the navigation bridge. Pressler, pistol at his thigh, looked up.

"All right, you barstid. You stay there. You can't come down or I'll kill you. You stay up there and rot, goddamn your soul. You'll beg me to shoot you, goddamn you. There'll be no water, there'll be no food, damn you—you'll beg me to put you out of your misery!"

XXVIII

November darkness comes early to London. Through the large, square windows of the fourth-floor office of Marine Carriers's London branch, Julie could see the glare of traffic and streetlamps glowing upward into the misty drizzle. Beside her at the large oval table that almost filled the spartan room, Mack—still partially on New York time—nodded affirmative to Lord Fensley's question. "Yes, I made the copy of the Rossi file myself. I can testify that it's true and complete. And the description of the *Stormy Petrol* sent by Mr. Raiford certainly fits that of the *Golden Dawn*."

Lord Fensley, the company's senior solicitor in London, wanted to be legally certain that the discovery of Boggs's theft and the *Stormy Petrol's* history, would withstand any challenge by the defendants. Probable cause as a requirement for a legal search was a concept relatively new to British law, still under-going definition, and an opposing counsel would certainly make use of all ambiguities. But Fensley saw the investigation into Rossi's death as a solid foundation to introduce—to Marine Carriers—the more important issue of motive for that death: insurance fraud and grand larceny. "I believe we can get by with your deposition, Miss Campbell." The man smiled warmly at her, the neat wings of his gray mustache lifting over prominent eyeteeth. "That way you need not appear in court in person."

And, Julie knew, it would also save Marine Carriers the expense of supporting a witness for a necessary though minor step in establishing the groundwork for a legal argument. She rubbed fingertips into her burning eyes and glanced one more time at her watch: three eighteen.

Mack, looking at his own watch, shifted wearily. He'd had no time to rest after his flight, and his face's gray flesh and day-old stubble showed it. "Can you call your contact in the Home Office again, Lord Fensley?" His finger tapped one of the many copies that had been made of Raiford's message to Julie. "Time—"

". . . is of the essence, Mr. Mack. I fully agree. I made that quite clear to our—ah—contact, as you term him. I assure you, he understands and my badgering won't contribute anything other than irritation." His smile at Mack wasn't quite as warm.

"Can he do it?" Julie asked.

"I see no legal impediment, my dear. There are clearly

established precedents in both national and international law. The substantive issues are coordination and logistics, aren't they? But we won't know his success until he informs us." He reassured her in a warm tone, "We've known each other since King's, and I have the utmost confidence in him, Miss Campbell. I'm equally certain your associate is faring well. He seems a most resourceful fellow—sending e-mail through a reserve modem—quite ingenious. I should like to meet him." He, too, tapped the copy of Raiford's message. "Damned fine work, that. Now"—he rubbed his slender hands together with a dry, brisk whisper—"it looks as though we could all use a bit of refreshment. I'll have some biscuits and sherry brought up. Do you prefer dry or sweet, Miss Campbell?"

XXIX

Raiford stared up at the gray clouds scudding overhead. He was almost beyond feeling the wind, now. The skin on his arms was taut and cold and stiff as marble. Once more he tried to relax his back muscles to control the spasms of shuddering that rattled his heels against the icy steel of the crow's nest. He must have slept sometime during the long, long night, though he could not remember anything but cold and the occasional gouge of the digital camera stowed in his shirt. Sunset had been a slow ebbing of gray light, and sunrise came just as dull and lifeless. It might have looked this gloomy to Alfred. Raiford hoped not. He hoped that Alfred at least had clear skies for his death. But Alfred, too, would have been thirsty. Very thirsty. Thirstier than he'd ever been in his life. Or would be. Certainly Raiford was thirsty. Thirsty enough to mutter curses when

Pressler, at early dawn, came out to the flying wing to call his name and toast him with a mug of steaming coffee.

Cold, too. Cold enough that bending his joints was an aching effort, and his hands—puffy and thick—did not want to close. But he would have to keep his mind off being thirsty and to ignore the cottony feeling in his mouth that made his tongue stick to his palate.

His lips twitched in a tight grin at the vision of Pressler lifting the steaming mug. "Oy—Raiford—to your health, man! A healthy but short life to you!" It was kind of funny. But it would be a lot funnier if it was the other way around.

Pressler had outsmarted him with the false announcement about the helicopter. He lured Raiford out and then swept the ship to nab him. Give the toad his credit. It was a trick Raiford would remember the next time he tried to escape from an oil tanker. Never go in alone; never go in blind. Well, he had, and here he was.

His dry, gummy swallowing was loud in his ears as he watched the bellies of the low, gray clouds sail overhead. Brighter, now. And maybe it was his imagination, but it felt a little warmer. Thank God it had not rained during the night. But a rain could slake his thirst, which he was not going to think about.

Below, staring up at him, an armed sailor stood guard. Probably Sung Ching—one of the crew that Pressler could trust. Maybe the one who had been with Alfred. And wouldn't it warm Raiford's heart to hear him bounce down the mast like Yun!

He would have to go down sooner or later. Pressler was right about that. He couldn't last much longer up here without getting hypothermic or delirious. Thirsty and very cold. Stiff. But as soon as he put a leg through the hatchway, Sung would sing. Might make it through one more day if the clouds kept the sun off. Last until dark, maybe. But Pressler would keep watch through the night, too. People he trusted. Sung. Shockley. Even Boggs, if necessary. Last night they had aimed the ship's starboard spotlight on the crow's nest, and all night Raiford had lain huddled from the wind and watched the radar screen just over his head flash in and out of the glare. It turned between four and five times a minute. Close to three hundred rotations an hour. Raiford had timed them. Shifting between imagined conversations with Julie and watching the radar screen. Flickering rotations as long as he could concentrate. Days as far back as he could remember. A summation of all his days. And to know that this cold, gray dawn could be his last.

He would have to go down soon. Be killed going down or stay and die of hypothermia. At least he wasn't in that cramped hole with the roaches. As he explained to Julie last night in the dark, he preferred to die out in the open under the sky. And that she, now able to take over Touchstone, should look for another partner. That thought was as cold as the wind that puckered his blue flesh, but he knew the truth of it. Life, in general, went on; his, in particular, might not. And he had no wish to impress on Julie or anyone else his will from the grave—no wish to condemn the surviving to live for the dead. Couldn't if he wanted to, so he might as well not want to.

XXX

After a conversation of short questions and long listening, Lord Fensley set the telephone back on its rest. His eyeteeth caught the light. "It's done."

"He's off the ship?" asked Julie.

"No, no, my dear. The arrangements to remove him from the vessel are done. The operation itself hasn't commenced."

"Oh." She sank back in the upholstered chair.

"A few hours more, a bit of luck, and we'll have him safe and sound." He sipped the remainder of his sherry. "We will, of course, wish to depose him as soon as possible. I've asked Reese to book an immediate flight from Cape Town."

"Has Wood been arrested yet?" asked Mack.

Lord Fensley's smile shifted meaning. "At half past. He was found at home in Staines and is being held for arraignment by their constabulary. I'm assured their process will take the maximum amount of time and that he will be held incommunicado throughout."

"May I?" Julie gestured at the telephone.

"By all means."

The information operator put her through to the police station in Rochester. Inspector Moore was still in his office. "What may I do for you, Miss Campbell?"

"It's what I can do for you, Inspector. A lead on the Pierce killings."

"Ah? Go on, please."

She told the listening ear about Hercules Maritime and the scheme involving the *Aurora Victorious* and the *Stormy Petrol*.

"Why didn't you give me this information earlier, Miss Campbell?"

"I didn't have the facts earlier."

"And you suspect this man in the Hercules office of being behind the murders? Wood?"

"Yes."

The line was silent. Moore either wrote or thought. "Your suspicions aren't enough to obtain an arrest warrant. But I will look into it. I ask that you stay away from any communication with Mr. Wood."

"He's already in custody at the Staines police station."

"What? On what bloody grounds? Do you realize the legal implications of interfering in a murder investigation?"

Julie held the receiver away from her ear as the tinny

voice squawked. Fensley, eyebrows raised, gestured for the telephone and dangled it in two fingers until the squawking noises changed into repeated interrogation, "Miss Campbell? Miss Campbell, are you there?"

"Miss Campbell has turned the telephone over to me, Inspector. I am Lord Fensley and I am responsible for Mr. Wood's arrest. I make no apologies for it. He has been arrested on valid criminal charges as well as to protect the life of an agent aboard one of the vessels with which he is in close communication. If you wish to lodge a complaint about those actions, Inspector, please do so with me." He listened to the reply. "Miss Campbell believed, and I concur, that you would want to interview Wood about your homicides. I suspect Wood knows a great deal about them. As Miss Campbell has dutifully informed you, the suspect is secure and available for your interrogation. And I will inform you right now that before I ordered his arrest, Miss Campbell told me nothing about a possible murder charge to be brought against the man." A brief pause. "Yes, that's right, Inspector. . . . Not at all—I will pass on your apology." He set the receiver gently on its rest and smiled at Julie.

XXXI

At first Raiford did not recognize the sound that ate into his now rambling conversation with Julie. It was faint and distorted by the strong wind, like the rapid flap of a pennant. Then it grew into a dull thud and he lifted his stiff neck to search the starboard bow for a moving spot that could be the flight from Cape Town.

"The bloody helicopter's here, Raiford. Come on down!"

Pressler's shout was followed by the pop of his pistol. The round stung somewhere close beneath the platform. Raiford peeked over the lip of steel to see the first mate say something to the guard, emphasized by the hard thrust of a broad finger toward the radar mast.

Tilted slightly against the strong crosswind and some two hundred feet above the slate-gray sea, a helicopter came rapidly from the west. It was larger than Raiford expected—designed for long flights and heavy loads—and moved fast. Instead of a bulbous Plexiglas nose, the aircraft had twin rotors and a capacious fuselage. Dull black, it held few markings and numerals.

At a distance, it circled once around the *Aurora* and Raiford's fingers played stiffly with the flare pistol. But any signal would be ambiguous. The pilot might even think he was being warned away, and God knew Raiford didn't want to make that mistake.

Slowing, dropping closer, the aircraft turned into the brisk spray thrown across the deck from the bow wave. Cautiously, it neared to hover over the peeling white *X* painted in front of the loading manifold. But instead of landing, it continued to drift slowly back toward the bridge, wagging slightly in the stiff wind as the pilot tickled its controls. Its rotors made twin circles of yellow blur that reflected in the deck's wet green. Then it poised above the slowly rising and falling ship as if timing its drop to the deck.

But it didn't touch down. Instead, two lines snaked out of the open doors in the fuselage and figures bulky with equipment and weapons slid rapidly down the ropes like dark drops along strings. They hit the deck and sprinted across the green steel and out of sight under the ship's island.

A landing party! Raiford watched as more figures wearing flak jackets and helmets dropped in pairs and dashed out of his sight. Then the helicopter quickly roared up and away from the vessel, the trailing lines hauled in by the door gunner as it swung aft the ship to dance from side to side, rising and dropping, never still enough to become a target as it hovered like a giant black seagull over the boiling wake.

Raiford peeked down at the wings of the bridge. Empty. The guard had disappeared.

Forcing his clumsy and unwilling hands to grip the icy steel rungs, he tried to hurry down the mast. But his numb feet kept slipping, and at one point he dangled by blue fingers as his plimsoles scratched for a purchase on one of the thin rungs. He dropped the last three feet, sprawling on the deck, his icy legs crumpling weakly. From the navigation bridge, he heard the crash of glass and shouted orders and the thump of heavy boots charging across steel decks. Then more shouts and a loud crack. An instant later, thick white smoke billowed from a deck below and the wind tore it into shreds and wisps of disappearing steam. Another garbled shouting and then silence. Raiford, shivering uncontrollably, stumbled for the ladder way, his eyes burning from tear gas.

XXXII

Raiford did not want to get out of a helicopter only to board another for a flight to Cape Town followed by a much longer flight to England. He was hungry, his joints ached, he damn near had pneumonia, and in the three hours since his rescue, he hadn't stopped shaking from the cold. And England in October had no place to get warm. He intended to go from Port Elizabeth to Cape Town, find a hot tub, and spend twenty-four hours slowly thawing in the warmth and flowers of spring.

But Marine Carriers insisted. Someone named Fensley repeated that the legal clock was running, and that the charges against Wood and the *Aurora*'s officers had to be filed or the suspects released. The information Raiford had sent was fine, the photographs he just e-mailed were spot-on, but his testimony as an eyewitness would be needed. They wanted him in person immediately, if not sooner, in order to craft the strongest possible legal case and to prevent the miscreants from fleeing the country. His flight from Cape Town would leave in four hours. He was further reminded that Marine Carriers not only paid for his rescue, but also arranged—through delicate and friendly contact between the South African, British, and Liberian governments—for Royal Marines to fly from Port Elizabeth to board the *Aurora Victorious*, which flew the Liberian flag. It had been to protect British property and British lives, as allowed by the slight twist to an old clause of international law: to wit, to guard a sailing vessel's crew seeking water or provisions, a nation's marines could go armed on any foreign territory without a declaration of war.

Raiford knew that the only British lives they wanted to protect were the ones arrested by the marines: Boggs, Pressler, Shockley, and Bowman. If any of the other officers had been involved, the ringleaders had not named them. The junior officers, who expressed shock and surprise but gave no confessions, remained to run the ship while waiting for additional officers to be flown aboard. Which, apparently, both Marine Carriers Worldwide and Hercules Maritime wanted. The very valuable British property the marines had risked their lives to protect still had to get safely to the Virgin Islands.

That was all well and nice, and Raiford was immensely grateful. However, his employer was not Marine Carriers but Mr. Rossi. Moreover, he was still shaking with cold, and he was not getting on that flight tonight. Good-bye. Three minutes later, Julie called to welcome him and to pull together the threads of the case. "The police have a lead on who killed Pierce and his family."

"Pierce? Pierce is dead?"

She told him about the massacre. "Inspector Moore said Wood spilled the whole story for some kind of break. Cooperating with authorities and so on. The killer's one Mark Rainey." Who, Julie knew, was a pretty good hand with a knife, as well. "They haven't picked him up yet, but with his record it won't be long."

"Did he kill Herberling, too?"

"Wood says he wasn't supposed to—that he didn't order Rainey to kill anyone."

"Right. He only told Rainey to whisper sweet nothings in their ears." Then, "Do you think Rossi was in on the oil theft?"

Julie paused. "I don't know. Maybe not. Maybe he was valuable because of his ignorance about tanker operations. Too new and too dumb to understand what was going on— that would explain why he was hired as third mate and his certification papers accepted without question." Her voice held a shrug. "That's what we can tell his parents, anyway."

"Let's leave out that part about him being too dumb. What about the sailors? When they saved my butt, they saved Maritime's stockholders a big penalty on the stolen oil as well as on the *Golden Dawn* claim."

"The company president, Eliot, said they'd get an extra month's pay."

"Thirty bucks?"

"Better than nothing. Oh—Mrs. Fleenor—remember her? Marine Carriers' agent who sold the insurance policy on the *Golden Dawn*? She had nothing to do with the theft. She had a settlement from some medical insurance squabble over standard versus experimental treatment on her daughter. That's where she got the money to pay off her daughter's hospital bills."

Raiford wasn't quite sure what Julie was talking about, but she sounded happy about it, so he felt happy. And it would become clearer when they finally got together and talked further. "Have they found the *Stormy Petrol* yet?"

"No. Mack says it's the *Golden Dawn* with a new name. Your description and the photographs fit perfectly. They've alerted harbor authorities from the Indian Ocean to the South China Sea. Mack thinks it might even be on a Bangladeshi beach, being cut up for junk. Oh, and the Brazilian liaison is waiting for Captain Minkey to show up in Rio." She asked, "When will you get here, Dad?"

"Not for a few days, Julie. I couldn't have lasted much longer, and I'm still thawing out. You rescued me just in time, sweetheart."

"That was Lord Fensley. He arranged for the marines to land."

"Just who is that guy?"

"Marine Carriers' chief solicitor in London."

"Thank him for me."

"I will." She added, "He's invited me to stay at his estate in Surrey until you get here. To look at his horses."

"To what?"

"Look at his horses. Since you're in no rush to come back to London, he said I'm very welcome to relax there with him until you arrive."

"You want to spend a few days relaxing with this Lord Whosis at his estate? To look at horses?"

"His stable has a champion stud. He seems quite nice. Lord Fensley, that is—I'll have to find out about the stud."

"A champion stud . . . and quite nice . . . Well, I don't feel so cold anymore. I can make that flight if I leave right now. I'll see you tonight!"

Julie smiled at the silent telephone and then at Lord Fensley. "He's over his chill."

EBOOKS BY REX BURNS

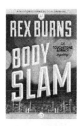
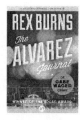

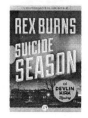

THe MYSTeRIOUS BOOKSHOP, founded in 1979, is located in Manhattan's Tribeca neighborhood. It is the oldest and largest mystery-specialty bookstore in America.

The shop stocks the finest selection of new mystery hardcovers, paperbacks, and periodicals. It also features a superb collection of signed modern first editions, rare and collectable works, and Sherlock Holmes titles. The bookshop issues a free monthly newsletter highlighting its book clubs, new releases, events, and recently acquired books.

58 Warren Street
info@mysteriousbookshop.com
(212) 587-1011
Monday through Saturday
11:00 a.m. to 7:00 p.m.

FIND OUT MORe AT:

www.mysteriousbookshop.com

FOLLOW US:

@TheMysterious and Facebook.com/MysteriousBookshop

OPEN ROAD
INTEGRATED MEDIA

Open Road Integrated Media is a digital publisher and multimedia content company. Open Road creates connections between authors and their audiences by marketing its ebooks through a new proprietary online platform, which uses premium video content and social media.

Videos, Archival Documents, and New Releases

Sign up for the Open Road Media newsletter and get news delivered straight to your inbox.

Sign up now at
www.openroadmedia.com/newsletters

FIND OUT MORE AT
WWW.OPENROADMEDIA.COM

FOLLOW US:
@openroadmedia and
Facebook.com/OpenRoadMedia